ALAN SHIVERS

Europea Halls

- A YA Slasher Novel -

This YA Slasher Novel is dedicated to all those 90s slasher movie lovers who grew up on "I Know What You Did Last Summer", "Urban Legend", "Scream", etc. We all deserve more chase scenes, so I hope you can get your fix here.

Foreword

TRIGGER WARNING:

As this is a Slasher Novel, there are many scenes full of violence, blood, gore and descriptions of deceased people. The book gets quite tense, which might be too intense for sensitive readers.

Viewer discretion is advised.

Acknowledgement

There are many people who have helped me along the way of writing my first novel. I had many questions, even more doubts and the following gems have eased the path to publishing "Europea Halls".

I'd like to thank Radu Muresan for designing the art work. I fell in love with your minimalist cover art, exceeding my expectations and vision on how the book should look like. A big thank you from Belgium to Romania.

Jenna B., without your editing, proofreading and honest feedback this novel wouldn't have been the same. Thank you for your time, dedication and eye for detail. This way America made it into Europea Halls a little bit too ;)

To all those early beta and ARC readers, for giving me feedback and pointers on where to improve. Much appreciated.

To my friends who have read early (very rough) manuscripts: Cleo, Lauren, Cameron, Raissa, Ellen, Rosie, Margaux and Agnes. Thank you for being so supportive and giving me the motivation I needed.

To my parents, who hate horror with a passion, thank you for dealing with my nerdy side and having nightmares after reading early drafts. I guess that's a good sign, right?

A very special thank you goes out to the extremely talented author Somme Sketcher. You've been one of my best friends for years and your professional insight has meant the world. I've bombarded you with many questions and you've stayed patient and helpful throughout the process. Your editing and feedback sessions have given me the drive to do better. I hope I did just that.

Thank you to everyone who has picked up a copy of "Europea Halls". I hope you'll enjoy the campy slasher ride!

Chapter 1

ALZBETA

It's one of those dreary, rainy Belgian evenings typical for January. Or, let's be honest, most of the year. The rain is violently hitting the window pane next to me in the living room. I notice some slight condensation on the windows, making it hard to see the forest outside. It's only just past ten, and it feels like the middle of the night. The wind is howling ominously outside, hitting the glass veranda ceiling with its sharp voice. I see these shadowy figures dancing, moving in an eerily elegant fashion. I realise they're only tree branches gently touching the veranda ceiling, but somehow, they still make me feel uneasy. Something about this night just doesn't feel right. Even though I'm home, a part of me doesn't want to be here. I look back at the ceiling and notice a dark, humanlike shape. Its right arm points towards the large stained-glass door. I squint my eyes and try to make out if this is actually a tree branch. My mind must be playing tricks on me, well, I hope it is.

A branch violently hits the ceiling. I look up in fear, but I can't make out where the sound came from. The wind seems to become less intense, at least for now. I exhale. Trying to ground myself, I sigh through the house's silence.

My phone buzzes. I jump, glancing at the chat.

MIOLAA group chat

Oliwia: You on your way, Alzbeta?

Lucija: We're waiting for you, girl! We need everyone here!

Matej looks up at me with those big, expressive green eyes. He tucks a dangling strand of his sandy blond surfer hair behind his right ear. He has been sitting on the red velvet sofa opposite me for a while now. The silence is getting to be a bit much.

"Is it the girls?"

"Yes. They are wondering where I am. I'm supposed to go out with them tonight."

This is starting to feel like a huge mistake. Matej shouldn't be at my house. "Listen, Matej, maybe you should go."

I can tell he isn't really listening to me. He is looking through the stained-glass windows into the forest. I'm not sure what he is looking at exactly, as it's pretty much pitch black outside, and the condensation is becoming more apparent by the minute. I look outside as well for a second.

"Maybe I should. Alzbeta, I just want to make sure that we keep this between us. At least for now. Can you promise me that?"

A pang of guilt blossoms in my chest. In a way, I wish my parents were home so they could kick him out instead of me.

"I—I don't know. Lucija's your girlfriend. She's one of my best friends. She needs to know; I don't want to hide anything from her."

I wish I could tell him exactly how I feel, but all I feel right now is confusion. I've never been the eloquent type. I've never

2

been a liar either though.

He glances outside again, lost in thoughts. So I do the same. I think back to when I first met Lucija, last September. I was immediately struck by her presence. She had just moved from Croatia into the dorms with us. Most girls need a while to acclimatise and observe before even daring to speak up. Not her though. She came in with this quiet confidence, this tall, red-haired girl with the perfect curls. She's the entire package, really. She just has this sense of cool—you can tell by the way she dresses too. Minimalist, she calls it.

I wouldn't call her cocky; she just seems to know who she is and what she stands for. She is one of those people you don't just want to be friends with, but need to be friends with. Magnetic might be a bit of a stretch, but I have definitely felt intrigued by her. I almost felt a sense of relief when we became close friends in such a short amount of time. We bonded over our love for anything vintage. I love strolling around the streets of old town Brussels with her, searching for the next little antique shop or looking up which flea market to go to next. Me, the small tomboy next to statuesque Lucija, roaming the streets. What I love about her is that she never makes me feel insecure. As much as I look up to her, I do have a sense that we're equals —all of us, really. I hadn't felt truly accepted before. In the past, some people looked down at me for being small. Others kept telling me "I look so cute in that sweatshirt" in the most condescending way possible. But with Lucija, it's different. I snap out of it and look at Matej.

"Lucija is probably wondering where you are. You should leave."

"If that's what you want. Will you be okay here by yourself? This house gives me the creeps." He turns away, staring at the

3

grand piano in the living room's corner, which has gathered dust. My mom keeps telling me I haven't practiced enough since we moved to Belgium, but I can't seem to find the motivation.

I notice his eyes are wandering off to the family portrait next to the piano. I guess it's not everyone's taste, these massive paintings with Baroque golden frames. "Ornamental," my mom would say.

More like pompous, I would reply in my head.

"Why, not used to luxury, are you?" I smirk, but instantly regret what I've just said. I should know better than to rub the family's mansion in his face like that. "Sorry, Matej. I didn't mean it like that. That sounded bratty."

"Self-knowledge is the beginning of all wisdom." Matej smiles faintly. I'm glad he can laugh it off.

"Just think about what I told you, okay?" He pauses. "I guess I'm off, then."

I look down and stare at the Persian rug that's like a fluffy little island creating much-needed distance between us. "Thanks for understanding, Matej. I'll see you at school tomorrow."

Matej nods. He walks up to me, and for a moment, I freeze. I think we both do. He takes another step in my direction, and I can almost feel the heat of his skin. The smell of his musky cologne mixed with the scented candles sitting on the mantle of the fireplace make me feel queasy. The dancing shadowy lights of the candles contour his angular face. As attractive as he might be, this light—or lack thereof—makes me want to take a step back. I suppose that would be rude. We decide to hug it out. It's not exactly a comforting hug. The moment his skin touches mine, I feel tingles running down my spine, but not the sexy kind.

My body is giving me clear signals that it is time for Matej to

4

go. I walk him to the main gate. I am a couple of steps ahead, so that I don't have to look at him. The moment I'm about to close the gate, he looks at me intensely. I know there's a lot more he wants to say, but I have reached my limit for today. I can tell he's gathering up the courage to say something, but I don't give him the chance. I quickly close the gates and mumble, "See you tomorrow then."

I couldn't be more relieved when he finally leaves. In a way, Matej is right. This house has always given me the creeps too. The creaky floorboards, the massive Renaissance ceilings, the little cherubs staring down judgingly every time I enter the hallway. I guess in a way, this house represents a new start to my parents. When we first moved to Brussels a couple of years ago, I never would have thought life was about to change the way it did. We never really had this kind of money before moving to Belgium. Back in Prague we were content with our little apartment. Life was simple but easy. Definitely easier than life in chaotic Brussels. God, I miss Czech food.

The TV on the first floor starts playing loudly. I jump up. I thought my parents were out. I'm sure I saw them leave. Oh God, did they overhear our entire conversation? The unease I felt earlier on with Matej around has only intensified. My chest feels tight, and my breath is becoming shallower by the second. I shouldn't be here. Not tonight.

"Maminka? Táto?" They don't reply. I am wondering where I last left the remote. It would be so me to sit on the remote without even realising it. But then, how could I turn the TV on when I'm on the ground floor? I call out for my mom again. "Maminka?" My voice is shakier than a second ago. I decide to walk up the golden spiral staircase towards the entertainment room on the first floor. When I open the door, I see the TV is still on, playing a video of our family trip to Singapore. I look around the room to make sure no one else is here.

It's just me. I try to recompose myself and take in the details of the room. Lucija told me once that if you feel stressed, look for objects with the same colour in a room. According to her, it will rewire your brain or something. Green—I'm going for the colour green. Red popped up first in my head, not going to lie, but I need a positive colour to calm me down.

The first thing I notice is the green carpet on the pool table on the left side of the entertainment room. What else? The green ball on the pool table, obviously. The accent wall around the chimney is also quite green. Vomit green, my dad called it once. Succulents, green. My gaze turns to the tiled floor in front of me. There are some hints of green in the Moorish tiles too. My mom did well with those tiles. I love the way the pattern creates some sort of cosiness in an otherwise quite austere-looking room. Then I see it—the remote is lying on one of the tiles just in front of the TV. The Singapore trip. I am taken back to the time when my parents and I were visiting those lush gardens, all lit up at night. I try to stay calm and reminisce about that trip, but I am already mentally looking for a way out of this house. I pick up the remote from the floor and turn off the TV. I stand here for a while, my breaths shorter by the second. My chest is really starting to hurt. Is Matej playing a prank on me?

The TV on the second floor starts playing. I jolt, screaming. It's the same video. I can hear my own voice, talking about the meal I'd just eaten on that rooftop restaurant in the centre of Singapore. The sound comes from my parents' bedroom. Something in my body seems to take over, and I rush towards the second floor, tightly grabbing the railing of the staircase. As

6

I arrive on the landing, I start second guessing my own actions.

Should I enter their bedroom? What on earth is happening? Is it one of those weird electricity surges I've read about? I hold out my hand, staring at the adorned door handle. *Just open it. What is up with you?*

I swing the door open and half expect to see my parents in a compromising situation, but there's no one in the room. I'm not sure if I should feel relieved or terrified. I try to play the colour game to soothe my racing mind and look for objects around the room, but I can't seem to calm down this time. Once again, the remote is lying on the ground, this time on the carpeted floor right in front of my parents' TV. When I pick it up, I hear the floorboards creaking on the third floor. I stay down for a second, making myself as small as possible. I stay in that position for a while, frozen with terror, waiting on the next sound. The creaking stops. I quickly stand up again and shut the door, locking it. My hands are becoming clammy as my palms slip off the door handle. I take my mobile out of my right pocket and try to send a text as fast as possible, but my fingers don't seem to follow my thoughts.

Alzbeta: *Matej, are you still here?*

No reply.

Suddenly, I hear footsteps right above me, coming from my bedroom on the third floor. I manage to stay quiet, but I can feel my heart is beating in my throat. My mouth is dry too, and it feels like my jaw is completely locked with fear. I look at my phone again.

7

MIOLAA group chat
  Alzbeta: *Girls, help.*

For a second I stop typing. Am I being dramatic? More footsteps. Nope. Definitely not dramatic.

MIOLAA group chat
  Alzbeta: *Call cops now, I'm home!*

No more noise is coming from upstairs. Should I just stay here? I could call the cops myself, but what if I get distracted? I need to stay focused. I know I can count on the girls.

The TV in my bedroom is turned on. I scream, even louder than last time. It feels good in a way, letting out all this tension that's stuck in my body. That damn video again. This time, I'm ranting about the humidity in Singapore. That's it. I'm out of here. There's no way I am going up the third floor when I should be going downstairs. I unlock and push the door of my parents' bedroom open and rush down the stairway. I notice the footsteps above me getting louder and faster. Not today; this is not happening today.

As I arrive at the entrance, I run to the main gate. It's locked. I used the key just a moment ago to let Matej out. *Where is it?* I fumble around for the keys, but I can't find them in any of my pockets. Great. They must've dropped out of my trousers when I bent down for the remote.

Maybe I should run back upstairs and check the entertainment room and my parents' bedroom. They could also just be lying on the table in the living room. Then I hear it again—the creaking floorboards. It raises all the hairs on the back of my neck. This can't be Matej.

8

I quickly look behind me. I notice someone is walking down the stairway from the second floor. Black boots. A long, old dark blue overcoat. I can practically smell it. There is something stoic, almost regal about the way this figure is walking down the stairs. I sense no hesitance whatsoever in the way he carries himself. My stomach tenses up as I notice he is holding a giant butcher's knife. This figure knows what he wants, and I'm afraid I'm about to find out what that really means. Before I can make out his face, I decide to make a run for it towards the veranda.

I run past the living room, quickly scanning the room for keys. *Nothing.* I up my pace and go to the veranda. I can hear the figure has reached the entry hall. I look up and notice the dark shadows are still dancing on the glass ceiling, almost mockingly. The stained-glass doors of the veranda aren't locked. I thought I had locked them earlier today. No time—I need to get the hell out of here.

Just as I open the doors of the veranda that lead out to the forest, I get a text message.

Unknown Number: *MIOLA.*

What? Who is this? What does the group chat have to do with all of this?
Right then, I feel it—this dark figure walking towards me, looking at me. The slowest pace. A part of me really wants to look back, but I have never been this scared in my life. I am completely frozen. I know I need to run, but—

He grabs my left hand. I let out the most intense scream I've ever screamed. I feel nothing. Then it comes rushing in all at once, the pain. As if woken from a dream I look at my hand and see the blood. I don't know how many seconds I stand there, looking at the stab wound in my left hand, looking up at this dark looming figure. *Could this be him?*

I instinctively kick the figure in the groin. Not waiting for a reaction, I slam the glass door into his face and run into the forest. I wonder if I actually hurt or even killed him. I did hear the glass door smashing. I need to get out of here. The neighbours. I see a light at the opposite side of the forest. That must be the Breinsteins.

I get another text. Startled, I stand still and take my mobile, trying to ignore the pain in my hand.

Matej: *What's going on? The girls are worried!*

Then I hear it: the soggy, wet leaves of the forest being walked on. The figure is right behind me; I can feel him breathing down my neck. I look back and scream as loud as I can. "David! Julia!" I run through the gloomy, muddy forest towards the Breinsteins'. At this time in the evening, the forest always looks mysterious and Gothic. Just dark, majestic branches looming over the city, hiding more stories than any of us want to discover. The figure is still after me, but he seems to be losing speed. I sprint as fast as I possibly can, past these massive trees and little ponds. I can barely see anything in this darkness—the wet branches keep hitting my face. The soil feels slippery, but I do the best I can. Just keep moving, straight on. Tree past tree. I can see their porch light; I'm getting closer. All of a sudden, my knees twist a bit, and my feet feel wet. I stumble. It takes me a moment to realise I have fallen down in one of the ponds. Luckily it isn't too deep, but I am still shivering from the ice-cold water. The stench of the rotten leaves in the pond makes me want to vomit.

I pull myself out of the pond and frantically look around me. Nobody. All I see is my own breath, like a misty grey cloud against the black outlines of the trees. Maybe I made it out safely. Maybe I outran him. He probably doesn't know the ins and outs of this forest the way I do. I just need to get to the neighbours' house and call the police.

A sudden sharp pain stabs my lower back. I drop down. As I try to breathe, I notice I cough up a bit of blood. It tastes like metal, like dirty old metal.

"Please, don't hurt me! I'll do anything!"

The tall, strong figure lifts me up. He looks straight into my eyes. Is that a mask? I notice the fiery eyes staring back at me. They look familiar, or at least I think they do. So much pain. The metal taste lingers in my mouth. He pushes me back down to the ground as if he wants me to make it out alive. Or, as if he's playing with me, toying with me. I get up from the soggy ground and try to run, but I'm not sure where I'm running to. My vision is getting blurry. *Is that them? Am I getting closer?*

Another stab. This time in my left leg. He seems to have hit a nerve, as the pain shoots up right to my head. An intense pressure pounds my forehead. I am not sure if I am still screaming or if the screaming is going on inside my head. I need to make it to the Breinsteins'. A bit further. I hear them — I can hear them. I'm sure it's Julia.

"Alzy? Alzbeta, oh my God, what is -? David, call the police!"

It's them; I've made it. Although my vision is horribly blurred, I can still tell Julia is running towards me. Sweet relief. I take a moment to breathe a bit deeper as I try to ignore all the pain I am in. My knees are shaky, but I am still here. David stands on his front porch, a bit frozen, on his phone with the police. I can tell by his body language that he is far from the usual cool, collected guy right now.

"Julia, help me! I'm being—" I look back at the dark forest behind me, but it's gone quiet again.

"I'm right here, honey, you'll be fine! David is calling the police. They will catch whoever did this to you."

"Can't you see him? I have no idea who—"

"Save your breath, Alzbeta. We will get you inside. I'll make you a nice cup of chamomile tea, and we will stay with you until your parents come home."

All of a sudden, Julia screams , "Behind you: watch out!"

The figure appears from behind the tree next to me. I feel a knife slicing through my spine, cutting through all the veins and bones. I hear Julia shrieking. I can't see her anymore, though. I can't see anything. I can't feel anything.

Chapter 2

LUCIJA

I had always watched these scenes in detective films where the next-door neighbour gets interrogated in the middle of the night about the passionate crime that had been committed next door. Never did I think I'd end up here. As I look around the interrogation room, I notice it looks almost exactly what I had imagined it'd look like. The harsh yellow walls are accompanied with the slight humming of the strip light above me that looks like one of those hospital lights. There's a water cooler in the far-right corner of the room too with a plastic cup underneath that looks like it has been there for far too long. Nothing about this place is inviting. Yet here I am, talking about the murder of one of my best friends. I try to ignore the damp smell coming off the humidity spots on the ceiling as I look into the detective's eyes and politely nod.

"Bonjour."

I look up, startled. "I'm sorry, I don't speak French." The detective seems a bit annoyed by me.

"I only moved to Brussels four months ago. I am taking classes; I'm just not there yet. I speak Croatian at home."

I notice I am rambling on. I always do that when I'm nervous. "No Dutch either, I suppose?"

I don't reply. Embarrassment is the last emotion I expected to feel whilst sitting in this cold interrogation room in the middle of the night. I don't know which other emotions I'm actually feeling right now. I guess I'm still shocked. Somehow it feels a bit like a dream. Like when you get out of anesthesia and you're not quite sure what's real and what's not.

"English it is." The middle-aged woman lets out a deep sigh. I guess the saying is true. People seem to treat you way nicer when you speak their language. Still, it doesn't feel like the time or place to be throwing snide remarks at me. My friend has just been murdered, and here I am, apologising for my lack of language skills.

The detective, Madame LeBeaux, is quite stern-looking, her blonde hair one of her pretty features. Her wavy platinum hair lays loose, long on her shoulders. Her telling blue eyes pierce right through me. This woman knows what she is doing. Those long nails are fierce too. She's actually quite hip for her age.

"So tell me, Alzbeta was one of your best friends, correct?" Her use of the past tense hurts. I want to correct her and say "is, not was," but I can tell I'll have to pick my battles with this one.

"She is—I mean she was."

"This group chat, MIOLAA. She sent you all a message, after which you called us."

"Right."

"Can you tell me a bit about this group?"

"MIOLAA is an acronym for our names."

"I see. Go on." LeBeaux diligently takes notes on her notepad.

"Eh, yes. It stands for Marieke, Ingvild, Oliwia, Lucija—myself—Ayat and Alzbeta."

14

"Continue."

"What would you like me to tell you?" I ask, genuinely wondering why she is so interested in our group chat.

"Tell me about your friendships."

"Well, it's all like quite recent for me. As I told you, I only moved here some months ago. The others have been friends for years. We all met at initiation night at our boarding school."

"You go to Europea, is that right? The private European school?"

"Correct." We are not all in the same classes, but we stay at the same residency at the boarding school. We all live down the same hall. Well, Alzbeta and Ayat go home to their parents' house quite often, but the rest of us all stay at the boarding school halls.

"And you are the oldest of the group?"

"No, I'm not. I'm 17. Ingvild is the oldest. She's just turned 18. Alzbeta is 18 as well." There's that present tense again. It all feels a bit surreal, talking about my friend group when Alzy has just been, I can't even force myself to say it.

"Oh, right. So tell me a bit about where you are all from."

"Can I ask why any of this is relevant information?" I instantly regret asking that question, as I realise how cocky it was of me to question the detective, who—in all fairness— I have warmed up to a bit by now. I have always appreciated strong independent women, but for some reason, I also butt heads with them a lot. I go on the defense, I've been told. I suppose that's what I've been doing here too.

"All of this is relevant information. The more we know, the sooner we can catch whoever did this to your friend."

I lower my shoulders. This is the first time I notice how tense I've been since walking into the room. I suppose she's right.

Pick your battles, Lucija.

"You're right. I'm sorry. I'm just like shaken up by the entire situation."

LeBeaux suddenly looks at me completely differently, her eyes full of empathy and grief. "I understand. My deepest condolences."

She couldn't have started off by saying that? I wouldn't have needed to get my guard up. I try to keep it together, but I know the tears are down there somewhere. It feels like they could hit the surface any moment now.

"So, I moved here from Split, Croatia, at the end of August last year to start the new school year at Europea. Marieke is Dutch; she's from Amsterdam. She is a year below me, but we have music class together for extra credit. You wouldn't say she's younger though. We call her 'Momma' because she is always the one who organises trips and she gets us all together. Whenever there's an argument, she's the one who calms us all down. She's the communicator, really. Oliwia is also a year below me. She comes from Poland, I think from a town near Krakow."

"You think, or you know?"

"I know, I know. She told me it takes her twenty minutes by train to reach the city. She's, I would say, the cheerful one. Always positive. She's really into films and series. I mean, most people are, right? But she knows all these crazy details about the directors, the lighting, the score, you name it. She's even in this movie club with a bunch of other people. Then the other girls are all in my class. Alzbeta, Ingvild, and Ayat."

"Start with Ingvild."

"Right. Ingvild is Norwegian. She comes from Bergen and she has opted for eight hours maths, like me. She's definitely the connoisseur of the group. She knows a ton about art and history. She and Oliwia are best friends."

"From what I have gathered so far from the other girls, it seems like you and Oliwia are best friends?"

That throws me for a second. What did the other girls talk about, exactly?

"Well, I guess I am the closest to her at the moment. She really took me under her wing when I first moved. She's shown me all the cool spots in Brussels and introduced me to the others."

"I see. How about Ayat?"

"She is Spanish and Moroccan. Apparently, she has dual citizenship. She is a bit more serious, like the studious one of our group. Really sweet girl, but her parents are like, super strict. She's almost scared of them."

I pause. Am I oversharing here?

"Is that the kind of information you are looking for?"

"It is, thank you. Could you tell me a bit more about the group dynamics?"

I raise my eyebrows. Tough question. "Difficult to answer that one, to be honest."

"Why is that?"

"We all just genuinely get along. We're all different, but somehow it just works. I know there are all those cliques that stab each other behind each other's backs, but -" The word "stab" comes flying right back at me. I feel tears welling up again. There they are. In a way, it almost feels comforting. I wasn't sure if I was just a monster, not able to cry over my friend's death. I have just been surviving, I suppose, rather than feeling and living.

"Here are some tissues. I understand this is all very upset-ting." For a moment, LeBeaux seems to want to hug me, but she retreats before getting too close.

"As I was saying, we actually get along. We try to empower each other and be there for each other. I would say we're all quite creative people. We're all into art and fashion. I guess we found each other that way."

"Do you think anyone was jealous of Alzbeta?"

"Jealous? No, I mean, I don't think anyone is above or below anyone else."

"Not even Matej?"

I look up. Why would she bring up my boyfriend? "Why, what do you mean?"

"Well, you do know he was texting with Alzbeta last night after he went over to her house, right? We have confiscated his phone, and he is being detained for the time being. It seems like he was the last person to see her prior to the Breinsteins."

"The who?"

"Her neighbours."

This is a lot of information to process. Why was Matej over at Alzy's? Is that why he hadn't replied to me yesterday evening? I am starting to feel a bit dizzy. I have no idea how to stay composed in front of LeBeaux when all I want to do is shout and cry. The thought of Matej seeing Alzy right before she died, I mean, it can't have been him. I know my own boyfriend. My throat goes dry, and I almost ask for some water until I remember the state of that plastic cup underneath the water cooler.

"What - what does it say on his phone? The conversation between the two of them?"

"I am afraid I cannot tell you at this point."

"Matej is my boyfriend. I have the right to know."

LeBeaux eagerly starts taking notes again. "Listen, Lucija,

you will know as soon as we do. For now, I would like to ask you to make sure you don't go anywhere on your own. And also, be careful with who you trust."

That's a bit dramatic. "They're my friends."

"There might be more to this story than we all know. You're the most recent addition to the group; don't forget that. There are surely things you aren't aware of yet."

"There are no secrets between us," I say firmly.

LeBeaux closes her notepad, stands in front of me, and stares me right in the eyes. I feel like she wants to make a point here.

"There are always secrets, Lucija."

Chapter 3

MARIEKE

How long have we been sitting here in the waiting room? It must be at least two hours in total. Lucija is the last one of us girls to get questioned. I wish I could be there for her, for all of them. I hate just sitting here, waiting.

"Marieke, could you not? Just for a moment, please," Ingvild begs as she grabs my right hand. Only now do I notice I have been strumming my hand against the chair.

"Sorry, I'm just so nervous. What is taking so long? It went way faster with the rest of us." I'm not the best at reading body language (or so I've been told), but even I can tell they all just need some silence. I play with my short black curls instead. I have a quick look at them. Should I go blonde? I feel useless. I am supposed to be Momma, the one who cheers everyone on, the so-called social glue (not my words, mind you.). I wish my actual mom were here right now. But apparently, Dubai is still her priority. Good thing we all live in the same hall. I would hate to arrive here in the middle of the night in Brussels centre on my own. I should call my mom, actually. What time is it in Dubai? My mind has been racing like this for hours. I've been thinking about everything and nothing, all at once. The moment I start thinking about Alzy, it's like something pulls me out of those thoughts. As if my mind is forbidding me to even think about her.

Oliwia's head is resting on Ingvild's shoulder. No idea how she dozed off, but good for her. Ayat just seems to be staring blankly ahead. Her eyes look swollen. I don't think I've ever seen her cry before. Other than those puffy eyes, she is still so well put together—even tonight, she is wearing Gucci. I mean, the rest of us all changed back into our casual clothing, so why is she still wearing the outfit from our night out? Even her bob cut still looks flawless. Compared to Ingvild's untamed long blonde locks and Oliwia's mousy (I mean sandy blonde; sorry girl) messy bun, Ayat has won the 'Who looks best at a police station in the middle of the night' prize. I know—me and hair. My mom has always said I should move with her to Dubai and become a hairdresser. I'd be glad if I made it through the year first.

I wonder what it felt like, being stabbed. Did she know she wasn't going to make it? *Girl, you're being morbid.* Sorry Alzy, if you can hear me.

The steel blue door in front of us swings open.

"Thank you for your time, Lucija. I'll be in touch." LeBeaux looks up at all of us. Oliwia is wiping off the drool from Ingvild's shoulder. "With all of you. Get some sleep girls; it's been a long night."

Lucija walks out to us, head lowered, and starts weeping. We all spring up and hug her. It feels like one of those moments you see in those old video clips from the '90s in which a camera pans around five girls in slow motion and shows how close they all are. The five of us all together. It should be six.

In a moment of spontaneity, I yell out, "Grand Place! We should go to Grand Place!" The others look confused.

"Why would we? It's 7AM." Ayat looks at me fully confused and semi-curious (or maybe that's just my interpretation). She's probably worried her parents would find out she didn't go straight back to school.

"Why wouldn't we? As if any of us are going to get any sleep after what has just happened. The sun will rise soon." I can just tell it's one of those chilly but crisp and healthy-feeling January days. It has finally stopped raining, and we all know you've got to make the best out of those moments.

"I don't see how you can still be positive and smiley. Alzy is dead," Oliwia points out dryly. I feel taken aback. That's not the usual Oliwia. But then again, none of this is usual. She sees how upset I am getting.

"I mean, sorry, Marieke, I know you mean well, but—"

"Why not?" Lucija interrupts her. "It's our spot, isn't it? In the middle of the square, in a circle. It's our thing. It should continue to be our thing."

I feel relieved Lucija understands where I'm coming from. She gently winks at me.

Here we are. Surrounded by gorgeously lit Gothic architecture around us. All the guild houses and their golden turrets with hundreds of years of history. Someone told me once Grand Place has the most gold in any square in the world. Looking around us, it isn't that hard to fathom. The big Christmas tree, donated by Germany this year, is still standing tall and proud in the middle of the square (One of the last days, probably).

We sit right next to it, as if the sixth member is still there in a way. I hate it when they take down the holiday decorations in the streets. But for now, it's still there.

Everything still looks cosy and inviting. The sadness can't hit me yet. Some hardcore early rise tourists with selfie sticks—is that still a thing?—walk around us, making peace signs in front of the imposing town hall. One guy tries to take a romantic selfie with his partner, presumably, but he trips on one of the slippery cobble stones. All the girls notice. We try to keep it together but burst out laughing once the poor guy walks off, face red like a lobster, trailing behind the embarrassed lady he is with.

We just sit here in silence. Usually this is our pre-drink spot, or the place where we catch up with all the gossip. Tea has been spilled on these cobble stones, let me tell you. But right now, the only noise heard is coming from around us. Ingvild is playing with one of the weeds popping out from underneath the centuries-old cobbles. She always does that when she's nervous. I like the feeling of these stones. There's something cool about sitting on stones that have so much history in them. Right now, they feel a bit damper and more uncomfortable than they usually do though. I wiggle my bum a bit and start to feel restless.

"Right, girls," I interrupt the silence. "I guess we should head back to Europea Halls; what do you all think?"

Ingvild looks at me and gives me a little smile. "Yes, Momma. I suppose none of us are heading into class. I mean, it's Friday. I think we can just sleep in, right? I'm sure the teachers will be understanding."

Oliwia agrees. "A hundred percent, boo. I just need to sleep off this nightmare."

23

Chapter 4

INGVILD

I look around the dorm halls. When I first moved here from Norway, I was pretending not to be impressed by it all: the large oak doors, the spiral case at the main entrance, the Baroque paintings hanging from those massive marble walls. There are Medieval tapestries on the third floor. Also, there's that massive library on the seventh floor full of original manuscripts of the first-ever Flemish texts. This place reeked of money, and I wasn't having any of it. In Norwegian culture, we just don't show off our wealth like that. We stay humble and quiet about all of it—false modesty?—until we die and have a bank account anyone would be jealous of. However, over time I have come to appreciate the opulence of this place. Everyone not-so-secretly dreams of living in dorms like this with girls from all over Europe. I love the mix of it all. Everyone brings their own food, language, and fashion from wherever they moved from.

Wednesday nights are my favourite. Last Wednesday, it was Sweden's turn. Swedish food (weird pickled fish, made me gag—not even going to lie), Swedish pop songs (I mean, Scandopop represent. I've always had a soft spot for ABBA and Ace of Base).

We usually pick out a folk song from our own language and translate it to the other girls. Sometimes some of the girls teach us some folk-dance routines that are always hilariously difficult. This upcoming Wednesday, it's supposed to be Czechia. Alzy had already been warming us up to the idea of Czech techno music.

I knock on Oliwia's dorm door. She opens up straight away. I can't help but smile at the superhero posters on her side of the room. Marvel, I should add. Reminds me of Karla, I wish those two could've worked it out. I look at her, and I can tell she's been crying too.

"Oh, Liv, come here." We embrace each other tightly. "Where are your roommates?"

"They've all left."

"All three of them?"

"Yes, they all said they wanted to give me some space, but I think they're scared of me or scared of being associated with me. Flaky if you ask me."

"So flaky! You shouldn't be alone. None of us should. Do you want me to sleep here tonight? I mean, it's a Friday night. The halls will be half empty—way too scary to be on your own."

Oliwia agrees without hesitation. "I'd appreciate that. Thanks, boo."

"This is the first time I am grateful we have dorm security. Nobody messes with those guys. We don't call them 'Arms' for no reason. The gun show is real with those dudes."

Within the next five minutes Ayat, Lucija, and Marieke enter Oliwia's dorm room as well.

"Here we are," Lucija says firmly. "I think we all have a lot to talk about. That Madame LeBeaux—"

Ayat grins. "Did she also tell you not to trust anyone?" The others laugh. It seems like LeBeaux has been warning all of us.

"I'm sorry. I know she's like a detective and all, but I'm not going to start distrusting any of you. She means well, you can tell, but she can be a bit dramatic," Lucija says.

"I agree. I know it sounds like a massive cliché, but we have to stick together," I reply. I notice Marieke is quieter than usual, at least for the last couple of minutes. "What are you thinking, Marieke?"

"I'm just—Look, I don't want to freak anyone out here. I am just wondering if this was a one-off. You know? Do you all think that whoever this person is that killed Alzy is coming after us too?"

Ayat looks up, startled. "Why would you assume that?"

"Well, because LeBeaux kept banging on about our group chat. It seemed like she was more interested in hearing about the six of us rather than finding the killer."

"I think she was just interested because she has to go through all the suspects, and because we're so close, that makes us suspects in her eyes, I guess. I mean, Alzy did text us to call the cops, so it makes sense they'd want to talk to us."

"But what if Marieke's right?" Oliwia asks Ayat. "What if this isn't over? I mean, the killer is still out there."

"Not necessarily." Lucija looks down at her maroon-painted nails. That girl knows her colours.

"What do you mean, Lu?" Ayat looks confused. I guess we all are. Lucija seems off.

"Matej is being held at the police station." Everyone starts firing questions at Lucija. I decide to take the lead on this one as I'm—let's be real for a moment—the more diplomatic, calm one of the group. "What does your boyfriend have to do with

26

this?"

"He - He was with Alzbeta just minutes before—You know."

"What? Are you kidding me? Why didn't you tell us this last night?" Whoops. So much for my diplomacy.

"I didn't have much information to go by. I still don't, actually. I can't reach him, because he is at the police station, and I don't have his family's contact details. What would I do anyway, call his mom and go, "Nice to meet you, I'm Matej's girlfriend; by the way do you think your son could be a killer?"

"Do you?" I look straight into her eyes.

"Do I what?"

"Think he could be the one who murdered Alzy."

"No. I mean - I don't think so. Look, my feelings are all over the place, okay? We've only been together for like two months, and I don't want to be that girl who just blindly trusts her man."

"Thank you!" Ayat erupts.

"I mean, I did. I did trust him, but why on earth would he go see Alzy when she was at her parents' place? They had the place to themselves. I'm not an idiot."

Oliwia interjects. "Do you really think Alzbeta would do that to you? Even Matej—we all know I have my reservations about him, but deep down, he's a good guy. I can't see him, you know." Oliwia hesitates.

"You can say it."

"Cheating on you. He's not like that."

Marieke holds up her hand as if she were in class. "Hold on here. I know what I am about to say sounds horrible, but given what has just happened, maybe Matej being the killer would be the best option?"

Lucija is getting annoyed. Careful there, Marieke; we all know where Dutch bluntness can get you.

27

"Excuse me? How is that the best option?"

"Well, he is at the police station, right? That means, if—and I am saying *if*—Matej did it, at least we're all safe."

"I hate to agree," I follow up, "but I do. I mean, we all watched *Scream* together last Halloween, right? The boyfriend was held up at the station too, and he ended up being the killer!"

"There were two killers though, weren't there?" Lucija asks me.

"That's beside the point here. Let's just hope the police figure all of this out before—"

Lucija stands, obviously irritated by the entire conversation.

"Lu, wait," I plead. "None of us mean any harm. The harm has already been done. We just want answers, like you."

"I know. I'm not angry at you. At any of you. I'm angry at myself. I want to hear Matej's side of the story too before I jump to any conclusions. I'm just—we all lost our friend yesterday, and in some horrid way, I wish we could take our time and focus on that rather than playing guess who."

Lucija breaks down. Oliwia jumps up and consoles her. Crazy how close those two have gotten in just four months.

Ayat swears loudly. Marieke is sitting next to her. "Why the foul mouth, girl?"

"My parents."

"What about them?"

"They are basically manipulating me into going home tonight."

"No way! We said we would all stick together. You know what happens when people split up in horror movies. I'm not allowing it. I'll protect you, you're safer here!"

"Sorry, Momma, but my actual mom is going to have a hissy fit if I don't come home. They are both worried sick."

28

"Back me up on this one, girls."

I immediately agree. "Absolutely no way, Ayat, you're staying with us. Tell your parents to come over here or something instead. Plenty of empty beds for the weekend."

"You know that's not how they roll. Look, I'll be over first thing in the morning. Maybe it's not the worst idea. Just, you know, being with them for the night, clearing my head. It's all been a lot."

"For all of us," I underline, "but I would hope we can all stick this out together."

Ayat is hesitant. She really needs to grow some backbone when it comes to her parents.

"My mom just texted me again. Her driver is picking me up in five. There's no reasoning with her; you all know that."

"Steve works during weekends too? Anyway, don't go, please."

"I'm really sorry. Just let me talk to them tonight at my own pace, in my own way, and I will make sure I can stay with you from tomorrow onwards."

The entire group seems unsure and a bit hurt.

"Come on, just for the night."

There's no response from anyone.

"Okay, I'm heading out. We have always said we would respect each other's decisions in life, no matter what. Steve is picking me up, and I am going straight to my parents'. I'll be safe."

That sort of softened me up. "You're right. Okay, come here. Give us a hug. Say hi to your parents from us."

We all hug it out and see Ayat walking down the hallway. She quickly looks back and waves at us before heading for the main entrance.

As much as I want to believe she'll be fine, something tells me she won't be. I want to stop her, but I also want to respect her. I know the way she is with her family, but something feels off about her leaving us.

What if she's next?

Chapter 5

AYAT

I know what they're all thinking. That I can't stand up for myself, that I'm too much of a chicken to actually speak up. Maybe they're right. I just need to go home, put on a soothing face mask, listen to some '80s music, and have a nice talk with my parents afterwards. They are the only ones who really know me. They're the ones who stood by me when everything went from bad to worse in Spain. Belgium offered a way out for our family. I wish I could just tell the girls what happened, but they're all so wealthy. They wouldn't get it. They don't know what it's actually like to move from house to house, hoping not to get evicted. The money only came once we moved to Valencia.

It's pouring rain outside—shocker. I stand by the main entrance, waiting for Steve. He should be here any minute now. That's the one thing I do miss about Valencia; the weather. I'll never get used to this 'four seasons in one day' in Brussels. The raindrops are getting thicker and more intense by the minute. I can barely see anything. Is that the limo? Ah yes, there it is— finally! The matte black limo stops right in front of me. Steve, you're a hero.

The back door opens automatically, so I hop in as quickly as I can, drenched from a mere ten seconds in the rain. My glasses are covered in raindrops; I can't see anything. "Thanks, Steve. It's been quite the day." He signals a thumbs up to me. At least I think he does. He better not be flipping me the finger. I'm such a blind bat without my glasses.

I get a text message. I do my best to read it, but it takes some effort with these annoying smudged glasses.

MIOLAA group chat
 Oliwia: "Be safe Ayat, text us when you're home!"

I text back at the speed I'm sure my grandma would.

 Ayat: "Will do, thanks for being understanding, all of you."

I still feel so unsettled by what has happened. I decide to shift my focus. I speak up, as I am seated all the way at the back of the limo.

"Steve, it must suck to drive through this. Are you okay?" He grunts. I mean, he's never been much of a talker, but I could do with a little polite conversation right now.

Another message.

Unknown number: *MIOL.*

I stare at my screen. I can barely make out the letters. Miol? I'm starting to feel a bit scared.

MIOLAA group chat
 Ayat: I've just received a text from an unknown number. All it

32

says is MIOL. What the—?

I hear a loud thump coming from the boot of the car. I jump up and look back. "Steve, did you hear that?" He doesn't reply.

Another thump. I hear someone's muffled voice screaming. Someone—someone is in the boot of the limo.

"Steve, stop the car. Someone's in the back—" For the first time, I properly look at the rear-view mirror. My heart stops. That isn't Steve. *Who is that?* All I can make out is some guy who looks quite pale with an eerie looking face. My mind starts racing.

The thumping gets louder and more frequent. I think I can hear someone yelling, "Ayat," but I could be wrong. The driver still hasn't responded. I need to get out of here now. I grab the door handle closest to me on the right, but it's locked. I try the other door handle on my left, but it's also locked. I look back up at the driver.

"Let me out of here. Who are you? What have you done to Steve?"

No response, just a stoic look on his—wait, he is wearing some kind of mask. No way, this isn't happening to me. I can't believe I blindly—quite literally—walked into the limo after what has happened to Alzy. The masked driver is still ignoring me. I wish I could read his body language, but it's as if there is no emotion, no fear, no guilt.

He slowly tilts his head towards me. I think I hear a faint evil laugh coming from behind the mask as he does. He starts driving faster. I can tell he is switching gears, but I have no idea which direction he is heading. It's not the route to get home, that's for sure. I try to look outside the window, but all I see are town houses and trees on big avenues. There are so many

33

of those in Brussels. I try to figure out what it says on one of the metro stops, but it's no use. He starts going even faster, slinging me from side to side in the limo, taking a sharp turn to the left. I scream and cry at the same time. I hear the tyres of the limo screeching against the wet pavement. He is losing grip of the road. Maybe if he crashes into something, I'll be able to jump out somehow. Or a red light—I'm sure he'll bump into a red light soon enough. There's more waiting than driving at times on these roads.

There it is. I notice a blurry red light in front of us. He slows down. This is my chance. As he stops the car, I grab onto the right door handle and try to break the window with my elbow, but to no avail. It won't budge , not even a single crack. I wish I had taken a cheap Uber; those windows would break in a second. I get dizzier and sweatier by the minute. The traffic lights turn green again and before I know it, we're in fifth gear, racing through the rainy streets of Brussels. I hear some car honks as we pass by a couple of smaller side streets. I look back at the driver and yell, "Stop the car. Stop it, let me out of here. I'm calling the cops right now!"

I grab my phone and notice how shaky my hands are. He abruptly stops the car. My phone falls out of my unsteady hands and slides under the seats in front of me.

I look around, but I still have no idea where we are. We're not on one of the big avenues anymore but on some dodgy little poorly-lit side street. For some reason, this location feels final. I feel a sharp pain on the left side of my chest.

"Please, just let me out!" I continue crying; I know this won't work. What other option is there? I look around me. No way out. I'm stuck inside.

The figure in front of me unfastens his seatbelt. He walks

34

out of the car and locks it up again, closing the door from the outside. I just sit here. I feel like I can't move. He is walking to the boot. His pace is steady and calm. He opens the boot. I hear the muffled screaming intensifying.

The figure grabs Steve, who has tape stuck to his mouth and his hands seem to be tied together. Poor Steve looks right at me, tears in his swollen eyes.

"Steve! Steve, get out, run! Get help!" I can tell he is trying to say something, but it all goes so fast. The figure is holding him from behind while looking at me through the back window. That sicko wants me to see what he is about to do. For a moment I think I recognise that body posture. Maybe Ingvild was right about the killer.

The driver pulls out a large butcher's knife, reflecting the taillight from the car straight into my eyes. I am blinded for a second by the glint of the knife. When I look back it's too late. I try to warn Steve, but I feel completely and utterly powerless. The killer holds up the knife and moves it towards Steve's throat, while still looking at me.

"Steve! No, run, kick him!" Steve tries to wiggle out of a death grip, but it looks like he has already taken some hits and he barely has any strength left in his body to fight. The figure pushes the knife into Steve's throat. He cuts across, the blood gushing like a river. The artery spews forth his insides. I scream. Steve's gurgling churns my stomach as I realise his vocal chords have been severed. I scream louder, for him, since he can't. My mind says look away, but my eyes refuse to listen.

I can't die like this; I'm not ready. I start kicking the window on my right with both legs, lying down and using all the strength I have left. It seems like the windows are budging this time. I try to use my high heels to their advantage. I will get out of here.

This is not it. I cannot let this be it. Some small cracks appear on the window. It's working. I look back at the boot, but I can't see the figure anymore. For a second, I pause. Where did he go? In the silence I can hear my heartbeat, the fastest it has ever felt. My lips taste salty as the sweat beads drip down my face. I lie down here, on the back seat, just wishing for all of this to be over.

My heart jumps when he opens the left back door from outside, instantly grabbing my head. I try to stand up, but in this position there's nowhere I can go. I can feel his rough hands. They feel like sandpaper. I shout as loud as I can. "Help! Somebody, I'm being attacked! Help!" The killer puts on black gloves. He smashes the window next to me into pieces - he clearly has more strength than I do - and grabs one of the large shards of glass. He puts one hand on my mouth. I try to bite one of his fingers, but he barely flinches. Then he grabs my chin and pulls it upwards. I try to escape from his grip, but I'm stuck. He brings the shard closer to my face. "Please, no! I don't want to die! I'll do anything!" I'm sure he can't even hear me, my muffled wailing barely audible through his firm grip.

I feel the glass cutting into the middle of my forehead. I hear this horrendous cracking sound as the shard cuts through my skull. The killer vehemently pushes from my forehead towards the middle of my nose. I feel like I am about to pass out. The blood starts dripping onto my glasses, which have been cut in two in the process. They fall off my face. I can barely make out the mask right above me, but right now I wish I was actually blind. The shard keeps slicing further until my nose is split in two and flops open to both sides. I can't see anymore. I try to scream, I try to move, I keep trying. I can't give up. I can't give in. I can't - breathe.

36

Chapter 6

OLIWIA

I look across my dorm room. I might be the drooler, but she certainly is the snorer. Ingvild is still in deep sleep. I'm grateful that she has stayed over again, 'cause my roommates certainly fled as soon as they could. I have a feeling they have been waiting for any excuse to flee, really. Ever since I came out to them. They had been acting all weird, throwing shady comments about my posters and why I'm, quote, "so girly yet like action films." As if one cancels out the other.

My girls reacted better than I could have ever hoped. I still feel myself around them, no special treatment. Even when I introduced Karla to all of them—not like that lasted very long, but still, it was real. I first met Karla at the Sundown Movie Club in Ixelles, in the south of Brussels. We clicked instantly over Marvel movies. Superhero marathons have never been so romantic. She tried to teach me some German, which in all honesty went way better than me trying to teach her Polish. She tried, but most people have difficulties with Slavic languages. She's the first girl I have ever said "I love you" to, and the first time I have ever heard it back too. It's moments like these when I really feel like reaching out to Karla. I believe there's more to our story. What do people call it again? Right— "unfinished business." We didn't exactly break up over a big fight or anything; she just wasn't at the stage in life where she seemed ready to be in a steady queer relationship. I know what I want and what I deserve, so I hope she gets to that point soon too. She was accepted from the get-go by the girls. That meant more to me than they'll ever realise.

Ingvild flings her left arm across the bed. She's the most dramatic sleeper ever. The deepest one too.

I don't get how she can sleep though. The past two days have been hell, the nights even worse.

I take my phone and start scrolling through some old photos. It feels like temporary escape from reality.

Great Gatsby night at Cirquito. I loved that night out. We all looked so cute. At the beginning of the night anyway. This particular photo, though—girl band vibes. Alzbeta rocking that suit and slicked back hair. I can't look at her for too long; it just hurts too much. Marieke with black curls we are all a bit jealous of. I did prefer her hair here. She shouldn't have chopped it off that much. That was our long hair era. Ingvild's green eyes pierce through the photo. She has always had something cold yet intriguingly inviting about her. I definitely couldn't pull off those bangs, but she works them. Her blonde long hair looks way more kempt than what I am seeing across the room.

Ah, Lucija. My girl. So glad she joined Europea in September. Don't know what I would do without her. She always says I'm her mentor, but sometimes it feels like the other way around. She knows all these wise Croatian expressions that don't really make sense in English, but somehow, I feel soothed when she brings them up. She is probably the most confident one out of

38

all of us; I just love that fiery side of hers. Goes with the hair. Don't mess with gingers; we have a fire in our stomach, she said once. Not sure if that was another Croatian saying, but it made me chuckle. Then there's Ayat. She has always had those model looks going for her, pristine looking, those deep dark brown eyes and that black Cleopatra haircut. I'm not sure I actually know the real Ayat though. It feels like she is hiding something. But I guess we all carry secrets.

I feel this overpowering sense of dread when I see her in the photo. Something about this entire situation doesn't sit well with me. Ayat should have replied to our messages in the group chat by now. Maybe she dozed off right after she got home, but I doubt it. No idea how Ingvild is asleep when we still haven't heard back from Ayat. I wish I had her parents' number right now.

I look at the time, 6:24 AM. No wonder Ingvild is having a chainsaw snore-off. The last two days have been a blur. Alzy gone, security guards outside our dorm room, parents and family on high alert. As if that weren't enough, there are journalists too, waiting for a glimpse of us at the entrance of Europea. I had always dreamt of being famous, but not like this. I thought I would be asked about my painting skills or being the first Polish superhero in the Marvel universe, not "how does it feel losing your best friend?" At least we might get some sort of answers on Monday. We were all asked to come into the police station to see LeBeaux again in two days. It might bring me out of limbo. This weekend is dragging. Ingvild looks up at me.

"Can't sleep, Liv?" She stretches her arms above her head.

"No, she still hasn't replied, you know?"

This seems to bring Ing out of her sleepy waking up phase. "What, are you serious? Ayat hasn't replied to any of the texts?"

39

Ingvild looks at me, hoping for some kind of reassurance.
"Nothing. I have a really bad feeling about this."

Chapter 7

MARIEKE

I stare at my photo in *The Brussels Times.* At least they chose a cute one. My curls are on point here; so is my makeup. (Rocking it, girl.) These headlines have been awful though, pure clickbait. "Eurocrats in mourning," "Europea tainting its flawless reputation," and more of the sorts. I didn't even give my permission for them to use my yearbook photo, but I guess that's how it works with the media nowadays. Our headmistress must be shitting bricks right now. She seems like a complete control freak, and this could seriously damage the school's reputation. I sound like my mom. She seems more worried about my future CV than how I'm actually feeling.

I look around my dorm room. My roommates are all still asleep. In a way, I'm glad they stuck around, but another part of me would like to be in the same room as Ingvild and Oliwia. It does feel good to have a bit of a breather from those dark conversations though. All we can talk about is Alzy and Matej. There haven't been any updates, so it seems like we're just rehashing everything and over analysing every single minute detail. I wonder what LeBeaux wants to tell us. Maybe they've found out who the killer is. I pray today can give us all some hope—we sure need it.

My phone rings. (Speak of the devil.) It's LeBeaux. I wonder if she's got any updates. I can feel my stomach churning, the nerves instantly kick in. I walk towards the bathroom and lock myself in so my roomies can't follow the conversation.

"Miss LeBeaux? How are you?"

"This is Marieke, right?" She sounds upset. My stomach feels a little tighter.

"Yes, it's me. What's wrong?"

"I'm afraid I've got bad news. I don't know how to tell you this, but—"

I know where this is going. My heart sinks. "It's Ayat, isn't it?"

"I'm afraid it is. I'm so sorry, Marieke. She and Steve McFella, her driver, were found dead in Ayat's limousine early this morning on the outskirts of Uccle."

I have a million questions, but somehow, I freeze. I can't say anything. It's too much to cope with. The tears hit my eyes and start flooding down with zero filter.

"Marieke? Are you there? I'm so sorry. The four of you should all come to my office as soon as possible so we can discuss what to do next. Will you be okay? The police officers will drive you. They're waiting outside your dorm rooms." There is genuine worry in her voice. It sounds like she is close to crying as well.

"I—thank you. I'll get ready." I hang up the phone. The bathtub I'm sitting in is cold. The entire room is. I cradle myself, trying to find comfort in hugging myself, but it doesn't work. The tears keep coming. Both Alzy and Ayat in just three days. "The four of you," LeBeaux had said. It doesn't even make sense. There are six of us. How can there only be four of us left? If two of us have gone, then who's next?

Chapter 8

OLIWIA

It looks a bit like group intervention, weekend edition. The four of us are seated in a circle with LeBeaux. Ingvild smirks and whispers "fierceness" to me. Lucija was right, LeBeaux's style is certainly above average for her age. She can put the quirk in quirky.

"I called you all back here to discuss Ayat's death. My deepest condolences, by the way." That feels like a bit of an afterthought.

"Is there anything we don't know yet?" Marieke asks impatiently and loudly. The volume on that one. On our way to the police station, we found out numerous updates online rather than from LeBeaux herself. It seems like the media is really hung up on turning our lives into a telenovela.

"Well, that's why you are all here. We found Ayat's phone in her driver's limo. She received a text from an unknown number saying "MIOL." This means the entire situation has changed. We are no longer talking about one single murder. Three people have been killed. It seems like we are dealing with a serial killer."

LeBeaux must feel like pointing out the obvious today.

"What you don't know yet is that we have traced the unknown number's location."

We all look up, suddenly interested.

"The number leads back to Split."

Lucija jumps up. "Split, as in Croatia, Split? My home?" Lucija always makes the corniest dad jokes about her hometown. "Split is where my parents split up." She told me once. I didn't know how to react to that one.

"Indeed. Do you have any idea who could be sending out these texts, Lucija?"

Ingvild shifts uncomfortably in her chair.

"Me? No, I mean, like, how would I know?"

"Is there anyone who might want to harm you or those close to you?"

Lucija sits silently, deep in thought.

"I really don't know. I mean, I didn't exactly have the easiest of lives before I moved here, but I don't see anyone actually hating me so much that they would, like, kill me and my friends."

"Not the easiest of lives. I see. Do you mind elaborating on that one, Lucija?"

The girls all look at Lucija. The only thing she has ever told us is that her parents fought a lot before they went their separate ways.

"Just the typical divorce. Like, my dad shouting at my mom, my mom manipulating me, me shouting at both of them. The usual. Right?" She looks at us for validation.

"A hundred percent." I say, sheepishly. How else am I supposed to react?

"So you moved out here with your mother."

"Correct."

"How is your relationship with your parents now?"

"Do we have to talk about this in front of my friends?" She turns red. "It's not something I usually talk about."

"Both Alzebeta and Ayat received a message from a number coming from Split right before they got killed. I think your friends here have the right to know."

"So it's my fault now, all of a sudden?" Lucija is working herself up.

"It's okay," I whisper to her.

"No, it's not okay!" She shouts back, more at LeBeaux than at me. "I'm just as shocked about this as the rest of you. I didn't want to get anyone in trouble. I have no idea what this person wants!"

"We know, Lu. None of us are saying or implying this is your fault. We've got your back," Marieke replies, oddly quiet.

Lucija takes a deep breath. "So—my mom and I are doing fairly well. I don't see her that much because she's often on business trips, hence the boarding school."

"Have you talked to her about all of this?"

"I have, totally. We have all talked to our families. She says she will come home in two days, and we are supposed to go on some sort of a retreat together. As if that will help."

"What kind of retreat?" LeBeaux asks curiously, writing frantically on her notepad.

"One of those zen things. Meditation, yoga, mindfulness. She is more into it than I am, I suppose, but I meditate too."

"I see. We have been trying to get in touch with your mother and your father, but neither has answered our calls so far."

Lucija snickers. "Welcome to my world."

"How about your father?"

"What about him?"

"How is your relationship with him at the moment?"

"I haven't seen him in five months, so I'd say great! We barely talk, if that's what you are asking. I don't like him."

"I see. I have to ask you Lucija —What about Matej? Have you heard from him?"

It is starting to feel a bit odd that we are all here. I feel for Lucija; she's getting the brunt of the questions. LeBeaux is on fire today.

"No, nothing. I don't know where he is or who he's with."

"As I have told you all before, Matej was released the morning after Ayat's death. We didn't have enough evidence on him to keep him."

"At least we know he wasn't the killer," Ingvild points out calmly.

"Perhaps not, but there is always the possibility of being an accomplice," LeBeaux refutes. "On top of that, why would he go into hiding if we have released him?"

"Is that question directed at me again?" Lucija asks.

I feel like I need to speak up here. Enough with all the tension already. "Matej might be scared. Scared of our reactions. Maybe he just needs some time on his own. He's not a bad guy! We know Matej. Perhaps he just can't face Lucija yet because he knows she knows he was with Alzbeta that night."

"Exactly. He still needs to explain to me why he was at her place. Look, I have no idea why he's hiding or dodging my calls. It just makes him look more suspicious. I don't know, alright? I wish I had an answer to all of this, but I don't." Lucija is welling up.

"Let me be blunt for a moment," LeBeaux starts off. "MIOLAA

with a double A turned into MIOLA with a single A, which then turned into MIOL. Do you get where I'm going with this?" she asks all of us.

"Yes," Lucija says. "It means that I'm next."

LeBeaux pauses for a moment. "It means, if the pattern persists, you could indeed be the next potential victim, Lucija."

For a moment I have a selfish, naive thought. What if Lucija gets killed and it all ends there? It seems like this killer is after her. What if she is the last one to go? I don't want that, obviously, but I just wonder. Could all of this be over soon? What if we can catch him or her or they right in time? Then another thought hits me. MIOL. MIO. I'm next after Lucija. My heart skips a beat at that realisation. If this killer is working his way down the alphabet, then Marieke will be the last one standing. All the rest of us gone.

"There will be extra police force around you girls at all times. I urge you all to delete the group chat as well. The less information that is out there about your whereabouts, the better. Don't tag any locations in any of your posts. Don't post anything to begin with. Make sure you stay together as well. Always. Do not go anywhere on your own. We will all be here to protect you, and I am on this case twenty-four seven. We are doing all we can."

We all look at Lucija. She must feel it. "Thank you. We will stick together." She looks at us, waiting for a reply.

"Absolutely!" Ingvild replies. We all firmly nod our heads.

"We are in this together," Marieke adds.

We all walk out of the police station quite shocked. I look at Lucija.

"You really had no idea about any of this? I mean, no clue as

48

to who could be sending those texts?"

"I swear, I wish I did. It all seems to lead back to me somehow. I feel so rotten that I have pulled you all into this situation."

Marieke looks up. "You couldn't have known! Besides, maybe the Croatian number is a coincidence?" I don't think she believes herself.

"Oh, come on, Momma, you're only trying to be nice. We all know this all links back to me somehow."

Ingvild starts walking next to Lucija. "Who then? An ex, an old friend, someone in your family? What could anyone have to gain from stalking us?"

"I need time to think about it," Lucija replies.

"What if we don't have time?" Ingvild asks quite bluntly. "We need to get to the bottom of this now."

I am starting to feel a bit light-headed. My stomach starts growling as well. I speak up.

"Girls, how about we go to CLØF? I could really use an espresso and something to eat. It might be quite busy on a Saturday, but it's worth checking it out."

Ingvild smiles. "That place. Reminds me of what I told you about—"

"Places that have Scandinavian vowels? I remember. It usually means it's an overpriced hipster place. But you've got to admit: their coffees are the best in town."

"It reminds me of home. Minimalist design and maximalist prices."

We all agree; time to have an attempt at a moment of normalcy and go to our usual coffee place. As normal as it gets anyway, with our two newly acquired policemen who are attached to our hips, it seems.

The moment we walk in we notice the crowd of young, hip

artsy people staring at us. I suppose most people in Brussels have seen our faces all over the news by now. I have to admit the newspapers haven't exactly been kind to us. Well, the comment section I should say: rich, entitled Europea brats, trust fund babies, EU bubble bitches. You'd think people would be more empathic to our situation, but it seems like a lot of people are too focused on money to actually care about what we're going through. I get distracted by the smell of coffee and vanilla. It hits me and brings me back into the room in the best way possible. Hans, the owner, nods as we walk in. "Your favourite spot is still available, girls" he says as he points to the far-right corner seats of dark green fluffy couches. The plants hanging from one side of the exposed brick wall, next to the pink neon lights, add to the charm.

"Thanks, Hans! Could I get an espresso and a large gluten-free bagel with cream cheese, please?"

"Coming right up. What about the rest of you girls?"

The others make their order. I am a bit surprised he doesn't mention Alzy or Ayat; he seems as cheerful as ever. Maybe he just wants to be kind? I could sure use a bit of kindness right now.

"Go ahead and take a seat. I'll come over in a moment with your order."

Lucija walks next to me and whispers, "How are things with you and Karla, by the way? Still, like, radio silence?"

This takes me by surprise. "Karla? I mean, I told you things became too complicated. Can we not talk about my love life or lack thereof right now? The moment she decides she is ready to be with me, out in the open, we can talk. Until then, I'm focusing on other things."

"But the two of you, you were golden. Really. You were the

one who told me everyone needs to come out at their own tempo. You said you can't push these things."

"I know that boo, but I had been waiting for months. I don't want to push her, but at the same time it's not fair on me either. There needs to be some sort of balance."

"Maybe when all of this is over, you can take her to the cinema and watch one of those generic superhero movies?" She winks at me.

"Did you really say generic? How very dare you!" I mockingly reply.

"Doesn't all of this crap put things into perspective?"

I hesitate. "What do you mean?"

"We've lost two of our best friends whom we both loved. Like, a lot. Do you still love Karla?"

"Lu, come one, I told you this is not the time."

"It's an easy enough question. Do you?"

There's no escaping this one. "I do. You know I do. I still think about her every single day. Even more now that we're in this situation."

"Then talk to her. I'm sure she feels the same about you. If you don't, I will personally write the directors of all Marvel movies to come up with a plan to get you two back together."

We both laugh for a moment. I nudge Lucija.

"Thanks Lu. You might be right."

"I usually am."

The moment we sit down, I take charge. "Alright girls, we have to talk about something."

"The Croatian number?" Lucija asks.

"That too, but I've been reading and looking up articles and YouTube videos on slashers." They all look at me with curiosity, or annoyance rather?

"I wanted to go back to when we discussed *Scream* the other day. It hit me, what if the killer is following a certain pattern?"

"Well, we know he is. The entire MIOLAA group chat pattern thing," Marieke replies.

"No, no that's not what I meant. What I mean is, what if the killer knows a thing or two about slasher films? You know, there's a certain structure."

Ingvild sighs. "Liv, I love you, but really? Everyone knows about those tropes. The First Girl is Alzbeta, the Final Girl- who knows? It all seems to point towards Lucija."

"Me? It seems like I'm next though. M is the final letter in the group chat, so maybe Marieke will be the Final Girl."

"That's the thing," I continue. "What if the tropes aren't necessarily followed this time?"

"You're saying the queer character lives for once?" Marieke laughs. "Sorry, my big mouth." She is starting to get on my nerves a bit.

"Thanks for that. But actually, maybe? Recent slasher films have gone against the tropes of the blonde feminine First Girl for example. Look at Alzy; not exactly Drew Barrymore."

"Wait, wait, I'm getting confused. Not everyone is such a film buff, Liv," Ingvild replies.

"Ha! Another trope!" Marieke laughs. "There's always the film buff in horror films. They usually don't last too long though."

"Christ, Momma, can you not—just for a second?" I am starting to lose it. "Okay, let's rewind for a second. In classic slashers there is, like you said, the First Girl, the killer boyfriend, the best friend, the nerdy film buff, the jokester, the Final Girl who is usually a virgin and a brunette."

Ingvild interrupts. "A virgin? We're all doomed then." We all laugh. It's a much-needed break. The tension has been building up too much.

"Sorry Liv, so according to the classic tropes, who's who?"

"Well, Ing, we know the First Girl; Matej would be the killer; the Final Girl would probably be Lucija, as the texts seem to point in her direction."

Marieke, not so surprisingly, interrupts me. "And the rest of us? We're all collateral damage? Kill by numbers?" She pauses for a second. "I'm done for too, aren't I?"

"Why?"

"Don't play dumb. The black girl. We never make it out alive either."

"Well, according to the old rulebook none of us do except for Lucija."

"But?"

"But maybe there's a twist in all of this. Something we haven't noticed yet?"

I feel bad for Lucija, with all this Final Girl talk directed at her. She looks at me.

"You're saying, what if I'm not the sole survivor? Or what if I die?"

"I don't know. I—I was hoping all of you could—"

"Could what?" Ingvild asks. "Help you out with this? Not even the entire Brussels police corps seems to have an idea of what the hell is going on. How could we?"

"Well, they don't know us. We do. We know each other. What are we not seeing?"

"So, if I don't end up making it to the end like I normally would, then who would?"

"How about all of us?"

"What do you mean, Ing?"

"How about we stop trying to study the rules and bend them instead? Why would we sit here discussing who lives and who dies? What's the use in that? How about we try to figure out where those Croatian calls really came from and where on earth Matej is? That's what we should focus on, not how woke or avant-garde the killer really is."

It seems like everyone agrees. Hans is coming to our spot. "I have your order ready girls; enjoy!" he says in his usual chipper voice, although his body language shows he senses the tension.

I take a big sip of my espresso. Nice and bitter. "So, how do we go about this? We can't just wait for the police. They're obviously no big help." I point at our two police guards standing outside the coffee shop, both apparently in stitches about something, with cigarettes in their hands.

Marieke shuffles to the front of the couch. "We try to figure out where Matej is. We are no detectives, so let them deal with tracing the texts. Let's talk to Matej's friends. Lucija, you talk to your family and old school friends and try to figure out who is behind this. We talk to anyone, everyone who could have some sort of clue about the killer. I'm done waiting."

We all are.

Chapter 9

INGVILD

I look around Liv's massive dorm room, contemplating how it all got to this. Just some days ago we were a normal bunch of teenagers, partying and "living our best lives"—words can't describe how much I hate that sentence. Why am I using it then? Anyway, the rest of the weekend was, as odd as it may sound, fairly uneventful. The rest of our Saturday, we basically ended up locking ourselves in our dorm rooms with the policemen standing right outside. I tried texting some of Matej's friends and Alzy's friends, but nobody could really help us out. Or so they say. Sunday was sadly not as uneventful. The bloody media kept trying to get inside the dorms, interviewing everyone that walked past by the main gate. The janitor seemed to look at it as his five seconds of fame and eagerly agreed to talk about "how tragic it all really is, those nice girls." I wanted to go out to the supermarket, but the policemen were strongly against the idea, and we ended up getting food deliveries. That's what usually happens on a hungover Sunday; this felt different though. Like I had no air to breathe. The entire thing feels rather claustrophobic. All four of us have been absolutely glued to our phones, constantly checking for updates or messages. The sad part is, we keep on reading all these updates—unless they're fake news—that LeBeaux hasn't even mentioned to us yet. Apparently, Lu's dad was involved in some money laundering back in Croatia, unless they just want to dig up dirt on her family. Who knows? I have the impression that we're finding out more through *The Brussels Times* than through LeBeaux. It's annoying, really. I mean, I like the detective. You can tell she's giving it her all, and she does ring us now and then to check in with us; but it seems like we're not getting anywhere. Like time has just stood still over the weekend. Going back to school today will be different—understatement of the year. I'm quite nervous about going back, surrounded by our bodyguards. Stepping outside of our "safe" bubble of the dorms feels risky. I'm sure people will be staring and giving us some kind of a misplaced pep talk too. I really can't be bothered with that right now.

I can't believe Liv's roommates just up and left like that. Cowards. I mean, I'm not exactly angry, as it gives me an excuse to sleep in the same room as her. It makes me feel safer. Not exactly safe, but safer.

I love the look of her dorm room, especially with some early rays of sunlight beaming in. I remember walking into Europea Halls at first and dreading the thought of sharing my space with three girls. As stuck up as this probably sounds, I'd imagined having a private room. I mean, it's Europea. My parents had hyped it up so much. The best private school in Europe, the best teachers, the coolest subjects to choose from (Human Sciences four periods, really? My parents need a reality check on what's cool.). But then, bunking up with three other girls? Until I saw the size of the rooms. I think most people's apartments can fit in one of our rooms. And then the interior. The two massive

Greek gold foil Corinthian columns in the middle of the room divide up the space into four smaller compartments, which still feel big because of those ceilings of up to five meters. Liv's room has by far the nicest chandelier I have seen in any of the dorms. I love the pastels. It's an original nineteenth century piece from Vienna, apparently. It all looks rather stately—quite the contrast with the movie posters behind her bed. That's what I love about this dorm. Each room looks like a mishmash of four styles, each girl anxiously trying to show her style and personality while being overpowered by the neoclassical architecture of the building itself.

My mom has always called me a geek—occasionally an old soul—and I guess she's right. I'm always the one in the group who notices the facades on the buildings as we head towards the next party. Them talking about how to smuggle in alcohol, me drooling over the frescos I see across the street. Without me I doubt any of them would even know the difference between Art Nouveau and Art Deco. Marieke has told me I should become an architect or an art historian. Either one sounds great to me. It'd give me an excuse to bury my nose in old stuffy books.

I do think I bore the girls with my fun facts at times, but they seem to accept me for who I am, which feels like a nice change. Most people in Bergen judged me a lot at school. Even my mom seemed to be disappointed I wasn't as cool or chic as her Scandinavian self. I look up at the Rococo-styled rosa around the chandelier. I remember telling Ayat about the odd mix of styles in the halls. She always listened eagerly to my rants about architecture, or at least I'd like to think she did. Lucija's right; she told us it felt so odd talking about Alzy in the past tense at the police station. Now Ayat as well.

My phone rings. Mamma.

57

What's that saying about the devil?

"Min datter! How are you darling? I read *The Brussels Times*—why didn't you tell me?"

"I was going to, Mamma. It's been a lot. If I see one more journalist at the school gates, I will lose it."

"But it's been days! Why wouldn't you tell me?" I pause. How honest should I reply to that one?

"Mom, you know why. It's just—it's tough on me, talking to you about this stuff."

"This stuff? Honey, two of your friends have died. I am worried sick about your safety!"

"Why aren't you here then?" I blurt out. No no, what did I do now? She'll want to come over. That's the last thing I need right now. I love her, I do, but her all of a sudden, trying to be close—or whatever this is—after her basically ditching me in Brussels feels fake. She is stumbling over her words. I decide to help out. "Sorry, I didn't mean it like that. I know you have to be there. Without your job I wouldn't be here, right? Diplomat world and all that."

"Right. I know it's been rough on you, the transition, but this is different. I wanted to tell you—"

This doesn't sound promising.

"I booked a flight. I'll be over in two days."

My heart stops. For some reason I feel a wave of gratitude and relief at the same time. I definitely didn't expect this. "Mom, what? You didn't have to." There they are, I had been holding them back. I hate crying in front of my mother. It has always made me feel weak. But right now, I couldn't care less. I just want her here. I need her here. "And what about Dad?"

"He is coming too, Ingvild. He will be there one day after I arrive. I wish I could hug you right now."

I can't reply to that, for the first time in days I can truly release what I've been holding in.

"We haven't been the best parents to you, have we? But God, Ingvild, I love you. So much. You need to know that."

"I know, Mom." But it's still nice to hear.

"How about security? How are these policemen treating you? Do they follow you around everywhere?"

I chuckle. "Literally, everywhere. Imagine how weird it is when they are standing in front of the toilet door, waiting for me to finish."

"Oh Ingvild, that's nasty." My mom laughs. "Are they at least handsome?"

"Mom!"

"Since when are you coy?"

"Still!"

"So, are they?"

For some reason I have zero filter on me today. "Yes, Mom, they're way too handsome. You'd be jealous."

She hesitates. "I mean, a man in a uniform."

"God, Mom, you're so gross!" But I can't help smiling. I've missed this. The banter, my English hallway girls would say.

I look up, it seems like Oliwia's shower was a quick one today. "Mom, Oliwia is coming back, I can hear her. I will text you in a bit."

"OK. Ingvild, can you please text me a couple of times a day? You know I normally wouldn't ask, but given the circumstances—"

"I will, Mom, I get it. I need to get going. Thank you for flying over mom. I love you."

Liv walks into the dorm room and looks a bit confused. "Did I miss any updates? It looks like you've been crying."

I feel a bit embarrassed at her seeing me like this. "No, it's just—my mom called. For some odd reason, all this pent-up emotion just came flooding out. I'm sorry."

"What are you sorry about? I've told you so many times you can always be yourself around me, boo." She gives me a tight hug. Ah great, even more tears.

"I know that. I just find it hard to cry in front of others. I always try to be the strong one in the group, you know?"

Liv gently smiles. "I do, but all of us know that there's a massive heart underneath all of this." She points at, I guess, my imaginary wall. "Look, Ing, we all need each other. You can't just take on the role of nurturer when you have lost two of your best friends. Besides, that's Marieke's role, or so she claims. You can lean on me just as much as I can lean on you. Deal?"

I'm glad to hear that. I suppose I do still put up a wall at times. "Deal. Thanks for that. Let's get ready for class."

Oliwia sighs. "Can't we just stay in today?"

"I think Marieke will be over soon. We should go, face our fears and all of that."

"But if we stay here, with the police outside at our door, we're safe. Why would we want to face the world when there's a killer out there who's after us?"

I stop and think for a second; she makes a valid point. I shake off that idea. "Because that's not living. That's not who we are, and you know it. We'll have those cops around us twenty-four-seven. Come on, let's go. We'll be safe."

"Famous last words," she half-jokingly replies.

Chapter 10

MARIEKE

It's 7:50 AM; time to go get the girls. I have been texting half the school to ask about Matej's whereabouts. They probably all think I'm a freak for posting stories asking for help. It's just that I hate not having control over things. And all of this; it's all out of my control. So I react the only way I know how—by being proactive. If I can't take care of myself, I can at least try to take care of my friends.

I look in the mirror. I'm not exactly sure why I'm trying to look cute, but I do. I put in a bit of extra effort today to bring out the curves with some bold prints and neon colours. Suits my loudness, Ingvild will surely say.

But that loudness has been subdued lately. There's this heavy iron block on my chest, just waiting to push a little harder and crash my bones into pieces. I've noticed over the past few days that it's all about motion. Once I actually get up out of bed, take that first step outside the dorm room, the rest falls into place somehow. But it's moments like these. Standing on my own in the room, the policeman waiting outside, looking at my own reflection. I see the colours, the curls, but I don't see myself anymore. I'm stuck. Taking that first step towards the door means handling another day. There's no such thing as normality anymore, nor will there probably ever be. (Momma's feeling deep today, OK?) I take a deep breath, nod at myself in the mirror, I even pull out a little wink (that was really cringe, why Marieke?), and open the door.

"Good morning, Miss Van Helder."

There he is, the guardian of the bloody galaxy. "I told you to call me Marieke!"

"Eh, I, apologies, good morning, Marieke."

I smile a little. Guess the loudness isn't entirely gone just yet. The policeman accompanies me as I knock on Oliwia's door on the second floor. She and Ingvild step out of the room instantly, accompanied by two more policemen. They both give me a tight hug and two kisses, one on each cheek.

"Morning, Momma!" Oliwia says, a little bit too loud to be natural, but I appreciate she's trying.

"Hey, you." Ingvild's not feeling it either today, I can tell. "Have you told Lucija we're ready?"

"Yes, she's waiting for us."

The three of us, or should I say the six of us, walk down the broad spiral staircase to the first floor. I can already see Lucija standing by her dorm room, accompanied by—you've guessed it—another policeman. I mean, Brussels could use all the police force it can get, trust me. This city is in dire need of it. But instead, they throw half their team on the four of us.

The moment we walk outside Europea Halls, the flashing lights hit me. Journalists everywhere. It seems to get worse each day.

"Marieke, Ingvild, Lucija, Oliwia! A moment of your time!" Before we can even say "No comment" or roll our eyes or do anything even remotely diva-like, the policemen step forward and take over.

"The girls will not be answering any of your questions. We have told you they need their peace and privacy. An official follow-up statement will be issued this afternoon," the oldest of the team says.

I wonder what the statement will focus on. The deaths? Matej? Us? They'll probably throw in more shade about how posh Europea is, as if that has anything to do with it.

For a second I try to pose for one of the photographers until Ingvild snaps me out of it. "Momma, don't smile at the photographers. We talked about this!"

"I can't help myself!" I giggle as she smiles back at me, nodding her head the way my mom does when I talk about hair. I cover my head with my left hand and walk past the line of nosies. Luckily the walk to the school grounds is only five minutes, but today I swear it feels like an eternity. I can see some classmates in the distance, glaring at the spectacle of it all. There are more parents around the school gates today too. Actually, a lot more. What's happening?

I see some Karen type holding up a banner that says, "Close Europea, keep our children safe!" Lucija notices it too. She grabs my hand. I can tell she is as nervous as I am. Then I hear the chanting. It's in French, so at first, I don't quite get it. Then it hits like a brick in my stomach.

"Close the school or keep MIOL out!" or something along those lines. I'm sorry, it sounds catchier in French, but that'll do.

This is why I shouldn't have left the dorms. Now we have an angry mob of parents on top of everything—great.

"Should we just go back?" Oliwia asks the rest of us.

"No way," Ingvild replies, determined. "I won't allow us to be bullied by some ignorant parents."

"Where did they all come from anyway?" I reply. "They all flew in with their private jets just to make a stand? Not today, sir!" I flip my weave and the other girls smile. I feel it, we all have some sort of fire in our eyes. We've gone through too much recently to let this stop us today. We all hold hands. Like a fire squad of four tough women surrounded by our sidekicks, we walk onto the school grounds. The wind kicks in at the exact right time to add a bit of dramatic effect to our hair. Beyoncé would be proud of us, undoubtedly.

The moment we set foot on school grounds, something shifts inside of me. I see all these different faces around me. Each one of them looks suspicious in their own way. Maybe it's paranoia kicking in, but my gut is telling me the killer might be lurking around the corner, waiting for one of us to trail off on our own in the hallway, a classroom, the toilets, wherever he can get us. What if this is Lucija's last day?

Chapter 11

LEBEAUX

I stare at the photos of Alzbeta, Steve, and Ayat taken at the crime scenes. So brutal. Where did that boy run off to? Why wouldn't he just go back to his parents'? The landline rings.

"Hello, Lebeaux speaking."

"Miss Lebeaux, it's Jan."

"Please tell me it's good news this time." My heartbeat starts speeding up.

"Potentially. Where are the girls?"

"I suppose you mean Lucija, Marieke, Ingvild, and Oliwia?"

"Yes. Where are they?"

"They're at school. I have just received confirmation from our team. We've sent four of our best men with them. Why, what's wrong, Jan?"

"I have been able to trace Matej's phone."

"How? What? Where is he?"

"He is on the move."

"To?"

"To the school grounds."

I stare at the photos again. "I will notify the corps immediately. I've got this covered, Jan. Thanks so much."

Matej—what is your game plan?

Chapter 12

OLIWIA

Ingvild puts her left arm around me. Here we are, under our favourite weeping willow. The tree sways a bit from side to side in a mournful winter dance. There's still a hint of frost on some of the leaves, glistening in the morning sun. The willow shelters us, with a hint of hope and brightness. This has always been our safe haven, providing shelter from the world when we needed it the most, but even this place doesn't feel safe anymore. The tree has been a part of the playground of Europea for as long as I can remember, but somehow not many students seem to be drawn to it, perhaps because it is tucked away a bit at the far end of the school garden. All the better for Ing and me, cocooning away through the seasons in our private nook of the playground. I pull my mustard yellow scarf around me a little tighter. The cold winter wind cuts through my jacket.

"Tell me what you're thinking," she interrupts the silence.

"This place. You and I. I've always loved this tree."

"Me too. I can sense there is a 'but' coming."

"But it doesn't feel safe anymore. Nowhere does. I mean, look at them." We both look at the two policemen sitting on the bench just across from ours who are studying our every move.

"I know what you mean. As if anyone can actually protect us. Why do they have to be men? Why are they always men?" She giggles and pinches my left shoulder. I can't laugh though. "What else is there, Liv? You're not telling me something."

"I mean, I don't know. It might sound stupid."

"Very likely, but go ahead anyway." The teasing, always the teasing.

"I was going to say, before you rudely interrupted me." I manage to force a little smile. "I don't get why Marieke and Lu would go to their extra credit class right now. I thought we said we wouldn't be alone."

Ingvild hesitates. "Well, we aren't alone really. We have those guys in front of us, and we're together, the two of us. They'll be back in an hour anyway."

"I know, it's just that Lu promised to—"

Ingvild sighs.

"What? What did I say?"

"Nothing."

"Don't give me that; what is it?"

"It's just, when was the last time we sat here, just you and I, under our tree? It's been forever. That entire discussion about the Final Girl and all that, it made me think: well, who's Lucija's best friend? The one who might make it out alive too? You are."

It starts to dawn on me. This isn't about the last couple of days. This is about the last couple of months.

"Is that what this is actually about?"

"What? I'm just saying I miss this." She pauses. "I miss us."

"But why would you miss us? We're always together."

"Yes, with the others. It's rarely just the two of us anymore. Look, I love that you decided to be Lu's mentor this school year, but you two have been spending so much time together that—"

"That what? Ing, just tell me." I feel a bit taken aback by all of this. Why are we having this conversation when Lucija, and, frankly, all of us, are in danger?

"I am going to sound really petty. Believe me, I am fully aware. But I feel jealous. Not all the time, okay? But sometimes when I see your stories on Instagram, and you're on another trip together, I feel jealous. I hate that I feel like that, and I hate to bring it up now, but I feel like we need to put everything out in the open. Definitely now. I'm not angry."

"Just disappointed?" I tease her this time around. She smiles, which feels like a massive relief.

"Smart-ass, no, not disappointed. I feel a bit hurt and left out in the cold."

I take a moment to let all of this sink in. At first, I was quite angry at her, but when I look at her now, I see she is genuinely upset.

"I see. Well, thank you for telling me this. I apologise if I have made you feel like that. I guess I have been a bit wrapped up in my own world at times with Lu."

"Apology accepted. I have to ask you something though. Promise you won't get mad." I feel the tension rise in my chest. Exhale, Liv.

"Promise."

"Do you have feelings for Lucija?"

"What?" I did not see this one coming. "Sorry, Ing, I love you, but that's actually quite offensive."

She looks shocked. "How is that offensive? It's just a question!"

"I thought you of all people would know me better than that. Just because I get close to a girl doesn't mean I automatically fall in love with her. She's not a rebound to get over Karla or anything."

She slowly takes her arm from my shoulder and meekly puts it in her own lap.

"Look at you and me, Ing! We are super close, we hug all the time; does that mean we have feelings for each other? Like, romantic feelings?"

Ingvild seems to finally get what I am trying to get across. Realisation kicks in. "Oh God. That was such a dumb question. I'm so sorry. I guess I got into my own head. Please don't hold this against me. I wasn't being—"

"I know, I know. You're not like that. I won't even start to compare you to my roommates, or should I say, ex- room-mates?" I look her straight in the eye. "I must've really hurt you for you to tell me this only now when the situation is this tense."

"Not on purpose, I'm sure. But yeah, I can't lie; it did hurt. I just miss you. It made me get all insecure and overly analytical."

"Let's do something together, just the two of us, once all of this is over, okay boo? Like, we can go on a trip together. We can take the night train to Vienna and take a Danube cruise to Budapest from there."

"I'd like that a lot."

"We can go see those Surrealist art galleries you've been talking about so much."

"I'd like that too."

We hug each other. I can feel Ing's tense body melting in my arms. I can't believe she'd been hurting this bad without me even realising it. When we glance back at the policemen, they quickly look away, appearing to watch the other teenagers on the playground.

"What do you think we're missing, Ing?"

"In our friendship?"

I burst out laughing. "No, you daft cow. I mean, we're still pretty much clueless as to who the killer is, right?"

Ingvild looks at me with those piercing eyes again. "It could be anyone, if you think about it. To be honest, I don't trust anyone right now, except for us. I don't even trust those policemen." She subtly nods at the men sitting across us.

"Really? Them?"

"Well, it would be quite convenient for one or more of them, wouldn't it? They follow us around everywhere and have access to the school grounds, the halls, wherever. I just don't trust a man in uniform."

"Even though you think they're hot?" I chuckle.

"Those two are not mutually exclusive," she replies jokingly. "What about you, Liv? Has your slasher brain picked up on anything you haven't told me yet?"

"I'm not sure. So many people with potential motives. The headmistress might hate our guts; LeBeaux has just as much access; the janitor too, with his skeleton key."

"What, groundskeeper Willy? As if!"

"It's always the one you don't expect."

"Meaning you?"

"Or you." A silence fills the space between us. I continue because I don't like this awkwardness one bit. "It could be any one of Lucija's family members back in Croatia. Maybe a jealous ex."

"And Matej?"

"He just seems too obvious, don't you think?"

"Perhaps," Ing ponders. "But then again, what's that saying? In broad daylight?"

"Are you quoting one of Lucija's Croatian sayings again?"

Ingvild laughs again. "I'm not sure. What I mean is, it could be someone who has been right in front of our noses this entire time. And no, I don't mean you, before you start that again."

"Then who?"

"How about Karla? Don't hate me now, but think about it for a moment."

"Karla? Why would my ex go off killing our friends and using a Croatian number? I thought you said the two of us are gold together? And now she's a killer?"

"You were the one who said there was something we weren't noticing. Maybe there's two or three of them working together. Who knows?"

I sigh. "I hope you're wrong on this one. When did our lives turn into a Gen Z version of *Cluedo*?"

We both laugh for a moment. This entire conversation is becoming very confusing. We're kind of joking about this entire "whodunnit," but at the same time, these are our lives, our friends. Laughter is also a coping mechanism, I've heard.

Ingvild lowers her head. "So, do you really think Lucija's next?"

Chapter 13

LUCIJA

The rest of the orchestra group walks off, some waving at us, most of them just full on ignoring us.

Marieke and I decided to go to music class together today. We just needed to find some sort of way back to normalcy. At least we were in a big group here, we both thought. There's safety in numbers, right?

The moment we'd walked into the auditorium, I instantly regretted our decision. All the stares, all the semi-genuine "how are you holding up?" chitchat annoyed me more than I could have imagined. Luckily, Mr. Ramirez read the room well and decided to get into Vivaldi mode before we even had the chance to properly reply.

I rested my violin on my left shoulder and transported myself into a different world. I have no clue if my skills were up to par today, but it didn't matter. It felt great. I think I even smiled. I could tell Marieke's cello skills were a bit shaky, but she stood her ground. Mr. Ramirez went easy on us, that's for sure. He is usually way more nitpicky, but today we went through the entire piece several times without him stopping us at every other bar.

I looked behind me a couple of times and Marieke smiled back at me each time. I'm glad we found each other through music. The other girls aren't that much into classical music, but to be fair to them, they do rock out to every single performance we have.

Mr. Ramirez walks off stage after telling us to "hang in there." To our surprise, Karel stays behind with us two.

"Aren't you supposed to be surrounded by an entire police corps?" he asks curiously.

I point up towards the doors at the back of the auditorium on the left side. "There they are. Always hovering around us." The two policemen are seated on the plush purple velvet chairs all the way at the back. It isn't exactly the opera hall from Zagreb, but it is still quite a beautiful auditorium. Definitely a change from my dusty old music room back in Split. I am not quite sure what Karel wants. I mean, he did hang out with us for like a month when he and Alzbeta were dating, but after that we would only politely wave at each other or talk about orchestra class during break time.

Marieke seems to sense what I am thinking. "So, Karel. What's up?"

Karel grins. "Direct as always."

"You know us Dutchies. We can't all be coy and beat-around-the-bush types like you Belgians."

"I'll take that."

He looks tired. I mean, I shouldn't judge, because I know I am not exactly looking my best, but I don't think I have ever seen him so worn out. He has dark purple bags under his deep brown eyes. His middle part seems a bit off today too, random strands of light brown hair falling over his eyes.

74

"I'm worried about you. About all of you. I mean, first Alzy, then Ayat. I can't imagine what you are going through."

Marieke looks at me. We both seem unconvinced about his intentions.

"Thanks, Karel. It must be tough on you too. You and Alzy had a good thing going for a while."

He looks down at the parquet floor, fiddling with his violin bow. "We did, but I know how close you all are. How are you both?"

Marieke looks at me again. I decide to answer first this time. "What do you think? I'm next on the chopping block. I am terrified. Absolutely terrified."

"I mean, in all honesty, I was surprised when you both showed up today for music class."

"Me too in a way, but what am I supposed to do? Sit in my dorm room with two policemen around me, waiting to, like, get killed?"

My stomach churns. All of this is still too intense to grasp. Am I really going to be next? "Life has to go on. It's the only way for me not to lose my sanity. We have protection all around us." I pause, doubting whether I should be this open to him. "You know, a part of me even feels like going vintage shopping today, just to—live. Do normal things. The shops are still open for two more hours. But who am I kidding?"

Marieke has a hurt look in her eyes. "You and Alzy used to go to the Marolles a lot, right? The antique and vintage area."

Karel has a faint smile on his face. "Oh right, I remember Alzy used to show me all these jumpers she had bought once. She was going on about how you've got the best eyes for vintage."

It feels a bit odd to reminisce so early on, but I suppose they both mean well. Karel senses my pain. Or at least, I think he does.

"So, why don't you just go shopping?"

"Walking around Brussels with bodyguards around me at all times? I'll pass. I'll stick to orchestra class for now."

"What about EU night? That's tomorrow, isn't it?"

I had completely forgotten about Czechia Night tomorrow.

Marieke replies. "Yes, it is. We still don't know if we're going. It seems a bit disrespectful to party when we have lost two of our best friends."

"Don't you think that's what they would've wanted?" Karel suggests. "For you to continue living, like Lucija was saying. The cops will be around too, won't they?"

"They will. I am surprised the head mistress hasn't cancelled the entire thing yet."

"Still no boys allowed?" He grins mischievously. That boy knows he's attractive.

"Why all this sudden interest, man? You know Miss Raven would have our heads if we smuggled boys into our dorms. You'd have to get past Arms too."

"You still call the security guards Arms?"

"Sure do. Anyway, nope, just us girls. Usually about thirty of us show up. Alzbeta had already started creating a Czech techno playlist."

I can't explain why, but this conversation is starting to annoy me. Karel is a nice guy, but all of a sudden, he wants to show interest in our lives? I'm doing it again. I wind myself up way too easily. My mom says I built up a wall after the divorce. I hate it when she's right. For some reason I tend to see the worst in people, especially guys. Matej isn't exactly disproving my theory either, where the hell is he? These girls are the only ones I truly trust. They've had my back since day one. I had never thought they'd be so open and welcoming to me. I know I don't exactly give off the warmest vibe, but with them it's been so easy to just be myself. I don't have to explain my whole backstory to them. The divorce, that weird family, all those fights.

I wish I could be a bit more like Marieke. Fair enough, she might be the bluntest of the blunt, but she's so effortlessly open and real at the same time. I feel like I still hide behind this tough exterior, worrying about saying too much or being too soft. Sometimes I want to just lay it all out there, tell my story, cry into all of their arms, and be cradled like a little baby. It's tough being tough. I wonder how they all see me at times. Well, we have talked about it quite openly, and it seems like they just allow me the space to open up gradually. It's only been about four months if you think about it. I can't be this open book just yet. But how much longer do I have?

Sometimes I do feel a bit insecure in the group. They've all known each other for years and I am still the new girl. They're all fluent in French and some of them are taking extra Dutch classes too with their private tutors. It seems like the girls are truly part of Brussels, even though we live in this separate little EU bubble. I still feel like I can't quite grasp this city. All these nationalities, these nineteen different communes, these bilingual street signs and billboards, these eclectic streets full of equally gorgeous and hideous architecture. At times it looks like someone just mushed a couple of towns together, hastily turned them into a capital, and called it quits: "You figure it out for yourselves now, peasants."

The girls have all tried to show and spread their love for the city to me, but I'm just not there yet. They've taken me on so many tours, taken me to the quirkiest little independent cinemas, shown me all the best coffee places. As much as they have accepted me and told me countless times that they love me, there's still this tiny voice inside my head wondering when they'll let me down. Or rather, when I'll let them down.

"Lucija? Earth to Lucija?" I look up at Karel.

"Sorry, what?" My head feels a bit dizzy.

"I said I have to get going. I just wanted to make sure you two are okay. Well, as much as that's possible given the circumstances."

The two of them started talking in Dutch for a moment, the perfect escape route for me. "Oh, okay. Thanks for caring. I'm sorry, I got distracted."

Marieke seems to feel bad. "Sorry about the Dutch. It's just nice now and then to speak our own language for a moment. I didn't want to exclude you, but it looked like you were off somewhere in your own world."

I smile. "You have no idea."

"You're right, I usually have no idea what you're thinking." Marieke smiles. Somehow that hurts me.

"Karel was just saying he was questioned by LeBeaux too. She was asking him a lot of questions about Alzy, obviously, and about Matej."

"Matej, why? Are you two still close?"

Karel hesitates. "We are, I mean, I don't see why we wouldn't be. We got over that fight ages ago. Before you ask: no, I haven't heard from him either. I have no idea why he went into hiding. Anyway, I really have to head out now."

Karel walks past the policemen and awkwardly says "hello" in a pitch far deeper than his actual voice. Why do boys always want to sound like The Rock? Marieke and I both grin at each other.

Marieke shuffles a bit closer to me. The two of us are the

78

only ones left on stage now, watched by these two protectors of the realm. Apparently, their names are Jan and Jeff, or Jean and Geoff—whatever. Their names sound like some characters from *Tintin*; how appropriate. We are supposed to feel grateful to have these men around, but I just feel trapped in this auditorium. Trapped in life.

As if Marieke can read my thoughts, she whispers into my right ear. "Let's go to the bathroom." There's a look of rebellion in her eyes.

"Why? You know those guys will just follow us."

"I know, but they won't go inside the stalls with us."

"So?"

"Just trust me, Lu." She smiles. Marieke signals Jin and John, waving at them. "Hello, excuse me? We need to go to the restroom."

One of them replies. "We will follow you."

"Thank you, sir!"

Marieke slams the toilet door behind her and exhales dramatically. She Marieke-whispers, "That feels good, doesn't it? A moment of rest!"

"Not too loud Marieke, they'll hear us." I actually-whisper back. "So, what kind of grand scheme do you have up your sleeve?"

She slowly pulls out a small brass flask in the shape of a heart.

"Cute! Where did you get that from?"

"Doesn't matter, shopaholic—it's about what's inside."

Marieke opens the flask. "I thought we could both do with some liquid courage today."

I have a sniff.

"Vodka?" I reply a little bit too loudly. "Are you, like, out of your mind? It's four in the afternoon!"

"Means it's happy hour somewhere in the world. Come on, don't go all judgy on me now. You're usually the first one to—"

I grab the flask out of her hands and take a big gulp.

"Easy there, tiger!" Marieke starts laughing. She puts her hands in front of her mouth.

"For once in your life, try to actually be quiet, Marieke. They'll hear us! Here, have a swig." I pass the flask to Marieke, who in turn eagerly drinks from it.

"Can you feel it?" she whispers. "That warm fuzzy feeling of freedom?" We both giggle.

"Are you girls okay in there?" John or Jim asks.

I put my right hand in front of her mouth. She continues giggling, her entire body shaking gleefully.

"We are. We'll be out in a moment."

I turn back to Marieke. "Let's just down this bad boy." We both take one more big gulp until the flask is completely empty. We both stand there in the tiny toilet stall full of graffiti and not-so-appropriate messages written in permanent marker, looking at each other, smiling, giddy on life. The headmistress had tried to warn us time and time again about the cleanliness in the toilets, but not even Europea can keep its toilets immaculately clean.

"So what's next?" Marieke asks.

"What do you mean?"

"Shall we continue the anarchy?" Marieke opens up the toilet door and points towards the fire escape at the other side of the restroom.

I feel like I know where this is going. "Marieke, no, seriously."

"Why not? Don't you want a moment of freedom? Let's just run out of here for five minutes. They have our mobile numbers.

We can ring them in a bit and tell them where we are."

"That sounds like the most stupid idea I have—"

"Five minutes. Aren't you tired of those journalists, the cops, the security guards? The fear?" She stops, I can tell her eyes are tearing up. "This fear, Lu, I can't take it anymore. Every single minute, living in fear. Being caged in, waiting for something horrible to happen. I hate being so passive. We're not like this! We're adventurous!"

I don't know if it's the vodka kicking in or the tears in her eyes, but I gently nod my head. "I can't take it anymore either, Momma."

Marieke's eyes light up. "So let's go on an adventure!"

Marieke opens the fire escape door with care - which is still far too clumsily in my book. She signals me to join her, so I do. Why the heck not? We step outside onto the landing and the cold wind hits me. So does the vertigo. I didn't know the staircase would be so narrow, nor that I'd be able to see through the grid pattern all the way down. We're on the fifth floor and suddenly this feels like a mistake.

"I don't know about this, Marieke."

"Oh, I forgot—you're scared of heights, aren't you?"

"Yes. Quite." I feel my knees are starting to shake.

"Let's run down. We'll be on the playground in a second!"

I look around. I can see a bit of the weeping willow at the other side of the playground. That's Liv's favourite spot, I remember. Nobody can see us from here, tucked away in the corner of the building complex. That's a positive at least. The last thing I need is the headmistress giving us a hard time. I look down again—mistake. The shaking sets in again. Marieke is standing next to me.

"Okay, you go first. I'll be right behind you. I've got you!"

81

she says encouragingly.

"Shouldn't you go first so if I fall, you'll catch me?"

"Just go already!" She not-so-gently nudges me forward.

I let out a little shriek. "Fine, fine!"

We both run down the iron staircase. We've crossed the fourth floor, we're onto the third now. We keep moving. Guess I won't be over my fear of heights any time soon. This is terrifying. I look back, Marieke smiles at me.

"Doing well, Lu! Just keep going!"

I can feel my grip on the ice-cold railing turning a bit slippery. Alright, just keep going it is. I continue down the stairs towards the second floor. My heartbeat is racing, but as scared I am, I feel quite exhilarated and alive as well. Anxiety and excitement are basically the same thing, except for the way our subconscious brain interprets the situation. It's official, I've turned into my mom. My fear of heights mixed with the vodka has made me lose my mind. I forget where I am for a second.

"Lu, wait!"

I turn around quickly. "What is it?"

"I think the policemen are trying to reach us. My mobile is ringing."

"Already? Just leave it. Let's get down first!"

"Maybe I should take it? Wait." Marieke quickly grabs the phone out of her fluffy winter jacket.

She stares at the screen. She turns pale.

"What is it? Who's calling?"

"It's—it's not a call."

I'm starting to get impatient; the less time on these stairs, the better.

"What are you talking about?"

"It's a message."

82

"Well, what does it say?"

Marieke looks up at me. "It says IOL."

All sorts of thoughts are running through my mind. The message doesn't make any sense. I'm supposed to be next. If it says "IOL," then Marieke – Oh God, not Marieke!

Marieke stands there, glaring at her screen. "Lu, I'm next. Not you. *I'm* next."

"We don't know that for sure, Momma. Come on, let's get down to the school grounds and find Ing and Liv. If we stay together—"

"We need to call the cops! Wait, let me call them." Marieke hurriedly dials their number.

Suddenly, the fire escape door next to Marieke swings open. Marieke screams. We both see it. The killer, standing right next to her, holding a pair of large garden scissors. The janitor? This awful emotionless mask staring at her.

"Run, Marieke, run!"

I run back up to go help Marieke, but before I can do anything the figure plows the scissors into her stomach with one swift move, her intestines spilling out. Marieke looks shocked. She tries to say something, holding her left hand up at me, but her intestines are falling out onto the stairway.

The fire escape door has been slammed shut again. Just like that, in what feels like a split second. We both stand there in absolute shock. The killer is gone. Marieke starts crying. I run towards her and grab her hand. It feels sweaty and cold at the same time. "Come with me, I'm not leaving you behind! Come on, we're almost at the playground, stay with me!" I pull her arm towards me. Now I'm crying as well.

"I can't, I—" The most horrific of sounds. The blood is leaking out of her stomach together with all other kinds of horrific sights. I forcefully pull her towards me, but Marieke drops down on the landing of the third floor. She crawls into the foetal position, cradling her intestines in her arms.

"No, Marieke, don't give up! I'm getting you help. Keep your eyes open!"

Marieke meekly whispers "No." Her entire body starts shaking, her eyeballs rolling upwards.

I hold her. I hug her. Tears roll from her eyes.

"Help please, someone! Help us!" But there's nobody to be seen.

Marieke closes her eyes.

"No, damn it, stay with me!" I rock her, I try to push her eyelids up, but she closes them again. There's a lot of blood. It's everywhere, it's on the staircase, on her, on me. A thick syrupy substance sticking onto everything it can get a hold of. Spreading like fear. Infecting all of us, one by one. I look back at her. She stops shaking and lets out a harrowingly long, creaky sigh. I stare at her face. I start sobbing.

She's gone.

Chapter 14

KAREL

Maybe Matej has been right all along. I finally understand why he went to Alzbeta first. He guessed she would know; she would have perhaps sensed something was wrong. I needed to see it for myself. I did. I'm sure of it now.

I pick up my phone.

Karel: Matej, dude, I think you were onto something. I believe you now. Please get back to me ASAP!

Chapter 15

OLIWIA

I knew the moment I heard the screaming at the other side of the playground it was Lucija. I thought it was *her*. I thought *she* was gone, not Marieke. Ingvild and I ran as fast as we could with the two policemen right behind us, but the moment we got to the stairwell, we knew it was too late.

God, the blood. I don't think I've ever seen that much blood, not in real life anyway. All the other kids started screaming and running away as fast as they could. They didn't want to be anywhere near us. I can hardly blame them.

I remember Ingvild looking at me and whispering, "It's Marieke. It doesn't make sense. The pattern. MIOL. It doesn't make sense, Liv."

I was thinking the same. It's as if this entire riddle of "who's next?" has overtaken our lives so much we don't realise what's real and what's not anymore. Marieke, one of my best friends for the past five years, lying there dead in Lucija's arms. How can anyone even really grasp that? How can you mourn the loss of a friend when you've lost two others just days before? When you're mourning your own life, you're fearing for your own safety? I wonder what the police will do now. They might put us all in quarantine together in some basement. Actually, I wouldn't mind that. There's not much else they could do.

When I read the live update on my phone, I have another realisation. I'm learning more about what is actually happening around me by reading the news rather than hearing it from the police.

Apparently, the headmistress has chosen to close down Europea for an undetermined amount of time. Basically, until the killer is caught, I suppose. I mean, I get it. The amount of pressure she must be under, with parents by the school gates protesting and her own students dying.

I just want this entire nightmare to be over. A part of me naively hopes LeBeaux will just do her goddamn job and catch the killer by the end of the day and we can all—I don't know— move on? My future therapy bill is going to be excruciating, if I even make it that far. One more day until we get to see our parents, finally. Just throw them in the bunker with us, please, so we're all safe.

Chapter 16

INGVILD

I'm glued to my screen, all these updates keep on popping up. It's as if I'm living my life through these news flashes. Or rather, I'm being lived. I look at the latest on *The Brussels Times* again:

Wednesday 11 January, 2023
  LIVE UPDATES:

- As more rumours start flooding in about the murders at Europea, more questions arise. Who is this Matej Dvorat? Where has he been hiding? His parents were contacted by our team of journalists, but they did not want to comment on any of our questions.
- Head mistress of Europea, Cynthia Raven, has decided to close down the entire school, including primary and kindergarten. 8000+ children are being sent home.
- On a surprising note, the head mistress of Europea has decided to leave Europea Halls open, as many of the students do not have their parents around in Brussels. As it turns out, 80% of the students have already left the halls. The

traditional EU night, held every Wednesday in the girls' halls, is allowed to go on with strict police supervision. Uproar by many parents ensued as they said it was "the perfect opportunity for the killer to strike." The director replied, according to sources, that there was "plenty of the police force alongside the halls' own guards, who will make sure that nothing will happen."

- Remaining survivors Lucija Horvat, Oliwia Kowalczyk, and Ingvild Aaberg were seen hugging each other as the coroners rolled out their friend's body. One student commented, "I've known them all for years. They're really nice girls, actually. Nobody really understands why this is happening to them at our school. This is supposed to be a safe place, you know?" When asking if the teenager would attend Europea's EU night, she replied, "No, I'm not. I don't think many girls will show up. I heard Oliwia, Ingvild, and Lucija are still going. Bit disrespectful if you ask me, but I'm not a judgy person."

- Europea's Trinity, as the survivors are now called, have been spotted at the local supermarket close to the boarding school. They were surrounded at all times by the police.

The past three hours have been a blur. Again. My mom hasn't stopped calling me either. She should be arriving tomorrow morning.

The nerve of those journalists. I've always prided myself on being cool and collected, but how could they just take photo after photo of the three of us crying? They've even coined us the Trinities or something, as if we're some country band.

Liv pulls on my right sleeve. "Ing, Ing!"

89

"What? Sorry, I was—"

"I know, you were out of it. I said we have to make a decision about Czechia Night."

"Why are we discussing this, Liv? We've literally just lost Marieke. Why would you even think about going out?"

"Well, it's more about staying in." Lucija chimes in. "We're locked inside these halls for God knows how long."

We all look around Oliwia's dorm room. It seems even bigger and more vacant than ever now there are only three of us remaining.

"If there are police everywhere and if Miss Raven for some reason is allowing us to have EU night, why wouldn't we? In honour of Alzy, Ayat, and Marieke!"

Liv does not agree on that one; she seems a bit pissed off. At Lucija? That's a first.

"Police everywhere? What good did that do for Marieke? They're useless."

We all look at the dorm door, knowing all too well the two policemen can hear us. Liv loses it.

"USELESS! Yes, I know you can hear me, and I don't care. Do your job! Protect us!" She stands up and runs towards the door. She swings it open and continues her venting. "How could you? All of you were supposed to protect us. We're innocent people! We're being killed, one by one! And you just stand there in front of our doors, doing NOTHING!"

John and Jeff are turning red. One of them awkwardly replies, "We are doing what we can, miss. We are so sorry about Marieke. We should've followed up on why they were taking so long."

"No."

Oliwia looks startled. Lucija is standing next to her.

"No, it was our fault."

90

I stand behind the two girls, looking at their backs, not entirely sure what's going on.

Lucija continues. "Marieke and I had decided to sneak off; they couldn't have known. I'm the one to blame here, not them." Lucija speaks in a calm yet defeated tone. The police officers look even more startled. I'm not sure they have ever had to deal with teenage girls before. I'm sure we're scarier than a drug gang to these poor guys. The sweat beads on their shiny foreheads seem to agree.

"You're doing your jobs, I know you are. I'm sorry we snuck off like that and put your jobs in danger too. I'm really sorry."

These men just want to run home as soon as possible; their body language is giving me constipated vibes.

"Thank you, miss, but it is our duty to protect you."

"Then please do—protect us."

Lucija pulls Oliwia back into the dorm and gently closes the door.

She holds onto Liv's hand. "I get it, Liv. I know this is hard, but we can't just lose our cool like that. We need to keep it together. Our sanity—we need it."

"She's right," I add. "Us shouting at people isn't going to solve anything. We are stuck inside these halls. We all know how quarantine can mess with your head. We've all gone through it with that bloody pandemic."

"So what are you suggesting, Ing?"

I take a deep breath. "What I am suggesting is that we should go to Czechia Night. Even if we go for an hour or so. I mean, I know we're all knackered. I might take a quick nap before we head out, but we need it. I mean, we went grocery shopping to get those Czech treats Alzy always talked about; we might as well go. You know, blow off some steam."

I get yet another live update ping on my phone. Oliwia looks at me, exhausted. "What is it this time?"

I take my phone out of my pocket and look at the screen. I'm shocked.

"Well? What does it say? EU bitches going down?"

"No," I reply. "It says Matej has been spotted around the school by some students."

Lucija looks up. "It says what? Matej was at the school when Marieke was killed?"

I nod my head. "I told you all. The killer boyfriend."

Lucija ignores my comment. "Then where the hell is he now?"

I feel her frustration. How is it that most of Brussels finds out all these updates before we do?

"Girls, what about LeBeaux?"

Lucija looks back at me, confused. "What about her?"

"We have her number, don't we?"

"Yes, your point being?"

"Why don't we call her up? If she doesn't have the decency to tell us what's happening, we have to step up and call her ourselves."

Oliwia vehemently nods her head. "A hundred percent! We're sitting here, waiting on who's next. That's all we've been doing. Waiting on updates, waiting on our parents to arrive. Let's call her!" She picks up her phone and dials LeBeaux.

"Put her on speaker, please," Lucija says. "I want us all to hear exactly what she has to say."

LeBeaux picks up almost immediately. "Oliwia? Hello?"

"Hello, Miss LeBeaux. You're on speaker phone. Lucija and Ingvild are sitting next to me."

"Are you okay? Are the police with you?" She sounds panicky.

"They're here, they're outside the door. We're in the dorms."

"Good, good. You should stay there until—"

Lucija tenses up her body, she is ready to pick a fight. "Until what? The killer strikes again? There are three of us left; three! We were six. Do you even understand that?"

A slight pause. "I—I do. I'm so sorry all of you have to go through this."

"That's not what this is about," Lucija continues.

"What is it then? How can I help?"

"Listen, I am trying to be as respectful as I can, but I think I can speak for all three of us when I say we are sick and tired of getting these news updates and finding out things before you tell us. You're supposed to be protecting us, helping us, but instead these journalists seem to know more than we do. It's our lives at stake!" Lucija is turning red; I don't think I have ever seen her this worked up. A part of me wants to console her, but this approach might be exactly what we need right now. How else would LeBeaux actually take us seriously? Funny how she was just telling Liv to stay calm. It seems like we're all at a breaking point.

"We need to hear everything. Every single little detail."

"You're—you're right." She stumbles, less stoic and self-confident than she usually is. I don't think she saw this one coming. "I apologise. I guess I have been too caught up in trying to catch—"

"Matej? Matej, who was spotted in our school? How did we not even know about this?"

"Not exactly on school grounds. Some students claim they saw him walking towards the main gate."

Lucija looks at us, even more angry. "Claimed? So now we have eyewitnesses, and you don't actually listen to them?"

"I did. We all listened to them. We have just finished the

interviews a moment ago, which is why I haven't called any of you yet. Listen."

"We're all ears." The sarcasm—you don't want to mess with Lucija; I can tell you that much.

"We were able to trace Matej's phone. He was on his way to the school, yes, but we ended up finding his phone thrown in the bushes two streets away from Europea, so we don't know if he actually made it inside. The school guards all state they haven't seen him at the gates, but obviously that doesn't mean he didn't get in some other way."

Oliwia straightens her back. "Wait a minute. You say he was on his way to our school. But how do you know it was him?"

"I'm sorry, Oliwia, what do you mean?" LeBeaux asks, with what sounds like a mix of curiosity and annoyance.

"You traced his phone. You didn't trace *him*, Matej, the person."

"But four students claimed they saw him."

"So now you *do* believe their statements?"

"What's your point, Oliwia? And I would appreciate it if you mind your tone." Oliwia's eyes open wide. She looks at me, signalling to Lucija. I get what she means. It seems like it's okay for Lucija to go off on a tirade, but the moment Oliwia questions LeBeaux, she gets defensive?

"My *point* is, maybe somebody either cloned or took Matej's phone and is trying to frame him. I mean, I'm not saying it's not him, but I've seen so many films where–"

"I will do the detective work here. You need to trust me on this one. Listen, I hear you. You make a valid point—you truly do—but for now, Matej is our strongest lead. As for now, we are focusing on him, but that doesn't mean we are excluding other possibilities or leads."

That seems to calm both Oliwia and Lucija. I take a moment and realise how calm I have been throughout this entire spiel. I guess that's what they mean with auto-piloting.

Maybe I don't have it in me to get this fired up. In any case, someone needs to keep their head cool.

LeBeaux continues, more calmly as well; "Lucija, I have to ask you something."

Lucija looks up at both of us, worried. "What is it?"

"You're the only one of the group who has seen the killer. I know you've given your description to the guards and the police corps, but did it feel like anyone you would know? Did the posture or size tell you anything?"

I'm dumbfounded. How have I not even asked Lucija what the killer looks like? I have been thinking about Marieke and what's next, but that description—it didn't even cross my mind.

"I've been thinking about that since—since Marieke died." Lucija lowers her head. All the tension seems to leave her body at once. She looks completely deflated. "I was standing a floor below them, so my perspective was all off, you know? All I can tell you for certain is that the killer is taller than Marieke, like about thirty centimetres or so, I'd say. But nothing about the stance or anything reminded me of anyone I'd know. I wish it did."

For the first time during the phone call, I speak up, gently: "Not even Matej then?" Lucija looks at me apologetically. "No, I'm not sure. It didn't feel like him, but I could be wrong. It all happened so fast. There was something about his eyes though. I mean, again, I wasn't exactly standing in front of him, but those eyes could pierce through any soul."

"What about gender?" I ask. "Are you sure it was a man? Did the eyes give anything away about that?"

95

"I'm not sure about anything. I feel useless. Croatian number, Matej, me not being able to save Marieke. I feel like I've dragged us all into this."

I can't console her on that one. Maybe after Alzy passed. But now, no.

LeBeaux answers: "I have to get going girls. I am getting another call. I promise I will keep you posted as much as I possibly can."

The moment Oliwia puts down her phone, she hugs Lucija tightly. Lu starts sobbing in her arms. Liv looks at me, signalling me to come hug Lu, but I can't.

"Ing, come here, come on!" Liv practically begs me.

"I can't. I'm sorry."

Lucija lifts her head and looks at me questioningly. "You can't what?"

"I can't keep on giving you sympathy, Lu. I love you, I genuinely do, but what you said to LeBeaux. I know I will sound bitchy saying this, but it's true. You *have* dragged us all into this. Not on purpose, of course, I know that, but without you—"

"Stop it, Ing, now is not the time!" Oliwia seems completely shocked by what I'm saying.

"No! I keep holding everything in, trying to play nice and keep us all together. They're not here anymore. Only half of us are left!"

Lucija looks at me with the saddest of eyes. "What do you want me to say, Ing? I'm sorry! I'm so sorry. I have no idea what is going on or how any of this even started."

"I know that! I know you're sorry, but I can't keep hugging you whenever you have a breakdown. They were our friends too, and we have known them way longer than you have."

Oliwia stands up and walks towards me. "Ingvild, stop it.

You're really being rude now."

"Am I? Or am I the only one who dares to speak up?"

"What the heck is that supposed to mean?"

Okay, guess I can get fired up when needed. "It means that you're just following around Lucija like a little love-struck puppy."

"This again?"

"I don't mean romantically, Liv, but all of us are suffering here, not just Lu. Listen, about Czechia Night. I need a breather—from both of you."

Oliwia grabs my left arm. "You're overreacting, boo. The dumbest thing right now to do would be to separate. Ayat did that."

"I'm just going to my own dorm room. My roommates are there. They texted me a while ago. I just need a rest. From all this." I feel tears coming up, but I stay composed. At least, I think I do.

"So you're not coming tonight?" Lucija asks, in a quiet, meek little voice.

"I am. I just need some sleep. I'll have a nap. I think I'm over-exhausted, to be honest. I will text you the moment I am up, and you two can come pick me up."

Oliwia doesn't seem to like the idea. "We need each other now, all three of us. Why don't we all have a rest here? We don't even have to talk."

"I love you girls, I do; I just need to have a breather. I will see you tonight." Before they get a chance to come in for a hug, I decide to step out of the room. I don't look back, because I can't bear to see the look on their hurt faces right now. My heart is racing. I'm all worked up. I'm not usually this dramatic, or at least I'd like to think I'm not. I know what I just did was harsh, but it needed to be said. The moment I step out, one of the policemen follows me down the hall. So much for getting some alone time. I look up at the ceiling and try to focus on the gorgeous Greek mosaics depicting different gods. The typical colours. Blue, white and gold. I find some peace in looking at the art, until I look into the gods' eyes. Their eyes protruding my core. Not even the art feels safe. It's as if all symbolism vanishes once safety is taken away from you. The protection of the willow, the art of the halls, what does it all truly mean when nothing can protect you? As I step down the long corridor, it feels like someone is watching me. There are too many shadows in this building, too much darkness. The killer could be hiding in any of these dark little nooks.

Chapter 17

LUCIJA

How did all of this escalate so quickly? Oliwia looks like she's seen a ghost. Ingvild is not the type to do a dramatic run off.

"Well, that was intense," I say, trying to lighten the mood a bit.

"Understatement of the year. I've never seen her like that."

"To be fair, you and I also turned into raging maniacs a while ago."

"A hundred percent."

"Liv, what did she mean when you said 'this again'?"

Her eyes are avoiding mine. I can tell where this is going.

"Something Ing said to me earlier today at the playground."

"Care to elaborate?" My throat feels itchy. I feel a bit nervous about what their entire conversation was really about.

She sighs and seems to doubt for a moment. "I'm not sure I should, but basically Ingvild asked me whether I was in love with you."

I'm not quite sure how to reply to that one. "Okay. And, I mean, how did—"

"My reply was no, if that's what you're clumsily trying to

ask." She grins at me. "I said I do love you, obviously, but not romantically. It seems like she's gotten a bit jealous about the two of us spending so much time together."

There it is again, another pang of guilt in my chest. "I've really messed everything up, haven't I? I don't need pity from you, but she was right. She was a tad bit tactless, perhaps, but she was like totally right."

Oliwia stares at the poster in front of her, not replying. Part of me is hoping she'll comfort me, but she seems to be stuck in the Marvel Multiverse.

"Liv?"

"I'm sorry, I don't know what to say. We all know you didn't ask for this. Nobody did. But I also don't want you to come between Ing and me. We should probably have a proper chat tonight, the three of us, and see how we can move forward. Once she wakes up from her nap and joins us at EU night, we need to make sure we hash this out." She sighs again and puts her hands through her wavy hair. I like it when it's loose like this— the bun can get a bit messy. "How did it all get so chaotic? We used to be such a tight group, and now look at us!"

"I'm sorry."

"Enough with that, Lu. We know you are. Adding guilt won't help now. This isn't your fault."

"Thanks. So, what's next?"

"We get ready for Czechia Night, put on Alzy's playlist and forget about the world for tonight. Although—"

"Although?"

"We should stay alert. Act three is about to start."

I smile a little. "Something tells me you're about to give me some fun film facts."

"You know me boo." She smiles back faintly. "Always the

trivia girl. Anyway, in slashers, usually the killer is revealed at some sort of party. It's always in the final act, act three."

"Right. Czechia Night."

"Maybe we should talk to the other girls and see if any of them seem suspicious or have any clues."

"How is that forgetting about the world? If we're interviewing people all night, we won't be able to actually enjoy ourselves for the first time in what feels like forever."

"I guess you're right. Be prepared, okay? Act three is usually where the bloodbath commences."

"That's comforting."

Chapter 18

INGVILD

The moment I walk in, my roomies get off the dark orange sofas and walk towards me. They can obviously tell I'm in no mood for talking, so they just hug me one by one. I've always gotten along quite well with Tammy, Aoife, and Themis, but they're no MIOLAA. Let's say our relationship is cordial. We've been there for each other when someone came back from school with a fail (usually on maths, because it's maths) or a new heartbreak. But telling them my darkest, deepest secrets? No, thanks, I've got my girls for that. Or I did. I can't bear the thought of losing Liv too. She's always been there. The thought of the killer even touching her makes me feel anxious, like I can't breathe.

"It's been a rough couple of days, right?" Themis asks with her sweet, Greek accent.

"You could say that again. What were you girls doing?"

"We were just checking out some guys," Tammy says with a sly smile.

I roll my eyes. "Are you seriously back on the dating apps? Aren't you supposed to be at least eighteen for those?"

Tammy snorts. "As if anyone actually checks that!"

"That freaks me out," I reply, "Who knows what kind of creeps are on there?"

"Oh well, it's just some harmless swiping. We're basically on lockdown in here, so might as well."

"Are you going tonight?" Aoife interrupts. She can clearly tell I'm not amused by wacko dating apps.

"To Czechia Night?"

"Yes, where else?"

"I mean, yes, I suppose so. Liv and Lu are going. I just needed some space from them. It's been a lot. I was thinking about taking a nap, but if it bothers any of you, I could—"

"No, no, stay! We were actually saying we could all do with a power nap before going."

"Oh, so you're joining me? That's nice!"

"Yeah, we figured you could use the company." Tammy winks at me.

I'm quite grateful to have them around me, but I instantly feel bad for Oliwia. Can't believe her roommates just left her behind like that.

"Thanks for being here, girls. What time is it even?"

"It's a bit past nine. How about we all lie down for half an hour? After that we could put on our pre-drink playlist and get ready," Themis replies.

I force a small smile. "I could use a little pre-gaming, sure."

A muffled thud sound wakes me up. I sit up and look around. The room is quite dark, but I can still make out some shapes. The streetlights are dimly shining through the purple velvet curtains. Some tiny dust particles float around the room, chaotically looking for a way to settle down again. The crystal chandelier—not as nice as Liv's—reflects some tiny slivers of

103

the moonlight outside. The girls are all still in bed. I look at my watch. 9:23 PM. So much for a power nap. What was that sound?

I look at the door and see a pair of feet standing in front of it. I notice the door handle being pushed down gently. I throw the cover over my body, lie down, and peek through the bed linen. My heart is racing.

As the door is opened, a bit of light from the hallway enters the dorm room as I see a figure lying down by the door. Is that the cop? I look up a bit and notice a dark looming figure with black boots and a long overcoat standing by the door. The killer. He's here. I should've stayed with Liv and Lu. The adrenaline starts flowing through my entire body. My bed is the furthest from the door, as it's positioned diagonally across the entrance. I am contemplating how to get out of here. Should I just run for it now that the door is open or stay still? Before I can make up my mind, I notice the figure walking towards Tammy's bed. She's still in a deep sleep, just like the other two. I need to warn her, but something inside me is stronger than I'd like to admit. I need to protect myself too. Before I can even think of a plan, the killer pulls out a large butcher's knife and stabs Tammy repeatedly through the linen bed covers. I am paralysed with fear. As he plunges the knife, I can hear her making some muffled, confused sounds, but she seems to be half asleep whilst being stabbed. *Wake up, Tammy, come on, wake up!*

Why aren't the other girls reacting? Oh no—they always put on their headphones so they can listen to meditation music. They have no clue he's here. Or perhaps they are pretending to be asleep.

I can see Tammy's right arm flopping down next to the bed, blood dripping from it in a small stream. This is the time to make a run for it. As I slowly start lifting myself from the bed, the figure starts walking towards the bed next to Tammy's, Themis'. I am trying to hold my breath as much as possible so the killer won't be able to hear me. However, every inch of me wants to shout and warn the other girls. I realise I am being selfish, but survival mode is taking over.

He aggressively starts stabbing Themis too. I can hear some small screams. God, she's actually awake. The killer is covering her mouth with his left hand whilst repeatedly stabbing her with his right. She's struggling, but maybe she can make it out alive. I know Themis is a fighter. She won't just give up. *Kick him, come on, do something!* My hands start shaking, it's like I don't know how to keep my body still in the midst of all of this. The killer quickly wraps both hands around her neck and starts strangling her. I see her body tremble underneath the covers. The jerky movements slow down. I can tell her body is giving up on her. I want to fight for her, but I don't know how. I feel a mix of anger, fear, shock, and frustration. It's like I'm locked behind a one-way mirror, seeing everything without being able to actually do something.

Themis stops moving. She's gone too, I realise. Two of my roommates gone in a matter of seconds. It is too surreal to even grasp. I try to catch my breath and slow it down a bit, 'cause the panic is really kicking in now.

That's it, either he walks over here or to Aoife's bed next. I let out a small sigh when I notice he walks towards Aoife's bed. That pace, so tauntingly slow. As if he's telling me he can take his time, he will get what he wants eventually.

This is it; I need to make a run for it. My body is fueling up with even more adrenaline, ready to start moving. The moment the killer plunges his knife into Aoife's body, I jump out of my bed and run to the door as quickly as I possibly can.

The killer swiftly looks back at me whilst stabbing Aoife. The poor girl glares at me as I run past her towards the door.

"Ing—please, help!" Her voice sounds hoarse, her teary eyes pleading for help. For a second, I stop. I want to help her, but the exit is right there. My only shot at making it out alive. The killer stares down at me as well whilst continuing to stab Aoife. I know those eyes. I just can't place them yet. The figure looks back at Aoife and in one horrifically smooth move, snaps her neck. The clicking sound makes me nauseous. Shivers run down my entire body, and I think I might vomit at any second. I continue running towards the door. He's right behind me. As I make it through the door frame, I smash the door right into his face, or his mask, rather. I hear a small grunt. I'm trying to make out the gender from the sound, but it's too muffled by the mask to tell.

I'm in the middle of the dimly lit hallway. Why is there nobody here? The moment I want to start running again, I trip over the policeman's left foot. As I drop down to the ground, my face falls right next to his. Dead. He's dead too. His left eye has been stabbed. His bloody eye socket sends more shivers down my spine. This time I can't keep it in. I hurl up everything that has been turning inside my stomach and let it all out.

When I compose myself, I scream again. "Help! Anyone! Help me!" but nobody comes out of their dorm rooms. It's only now that I realise Czechia Night has already started. Most girls usually arrive on time, so they're probably all at the lounge on the fourth floor. I stand up again, still quite wobbly and weak to my knees, and run down the long hallway.

The killer throws the door back open and runs right behind me.

I can tell he's faster than me. I just need to make it to the lounge room—there will be policemen there. As I run along all those pieces of art around me, it feels like these paintings are staring at me, judging me with their condescending glares. I'm almost at the spiral staircase, but he's getting closer. Way too close. The killer grabs my right leg and stabs it. I can feel the knife sliding through my leg, moving downwards, touching my bones and flesh. A horribly sharp pain. I let out yet another scream and kick him back with my other leg. He loses his balance for a second and fumbles backwards. I can't believe nobody can hear this. I try to run up the staircase, but I know I'm moving too slowly because of my limp. I look back and see the killer is patiently walking behind me again, up the staircase, waiting for me to give up.

"Leave me alone! Who are you? Matej? Leave me the hell alone!" I start crying. The pain intensifies.

Just ten more steps and I'll be on the third floor. It's too much, this pain. I pull my leg up with both hands. Nine more steps. The killer is just a couple of steps behind me, probably enjoying my pain, that sick freak. Eight more steps and I can be with my girls; I need them now. Seven. The killer puts his knife on the railing. It makes the most unnerving screeching metal noise. Six more steps. I can't give up now; I've come too far over the past couple of days. I can feel the fabric of the killer's overcoat gently touching my left leg. I yelp and jump quickly, five, four more steps. I want to look behind me, but I know I shouldn't, so I just keep moving. Three steps, you've got this, Ingvild. I'm not becoming a letter in his alphabet. Two more steps, I am trying to reach for the landing, one more step. I use all the strength left in me. I make it to the landing of the hallway but immediately drop down. I don't know how much I've got left in me. The figure steps towards me and leans over me. I am looking straight at the mask. He pulls out the knife.

"Someone please help! The killer is here!"

To my surprise, Diana, the girl from my bio class, swings open her dorm door. "Ingvild? Oh my God, what's happening?" She looks petrified.

"Diana, call for help!"

The killer stands up straight again and looks right into Diana's eyes. Diana screams and tries to run back into her room, but the killer is faster. So damn fast. He grabs Diana's arm and pulls her towards him. Poor Diana; this is all my fault. With every inch of fighting spirit left in me, I pull myself up and stumble towards the cinema room. I can tell the killer is fully focused on Diana, as he keeps stabbing her stomach. She looks at me for a second, but I have to look away. The pain in her eyes is too much to cope with.

The cinema room is two doors down from Diana's room. As I lower the crooked door handle, I see the killer is still not looking at me. I quickly open the door, hop in and quietly shut it behind me.

A moment of peace. I put my right hand on my heart and take some deep breaths. I try to connect with my body. My heartbeat is finally slowing down. I try to ignore the pain, but sharp pains shoot through my spine. Maybe I'll make it through; I've made it this far. I look around the cinema room, which is almost as dark as my own dorm room was a moment ago. I can make out the seats and the screen in the room, as one of the curtains hasn't been closed properly and a beam of moonlight is shining through. We usually watch documentaries or indie flicks in here that our teachers make us analyse and write essays on. I look at the back row, where the six of us used to sit together. A wave of sadness hits me. Whatever will happen next, things just won't be the same again.

I decide to hide under some of the seats in the middle of the left side of the room, facing the projection screen. There are about twenty rows of cinema chairs, so I stumble towards the middle row and lie down on the ground, between the chairs. The killer might not know I'm in here. I don't think he actually saw me come in. I might be okay. Think Ing, think; what's next? The sharp pain comes back with a vengeance. I can tell I'm sweating profusely. I feel hot and cold at the same time. Your phone. Your phone. Text the girls.

I pull out my phone and look for the MIOLAA group chat. It takes me a second to realise it doesn't exist anymore. I decide to text Oliwia instead. As I start typing in her name, I receive a message.

Unknown Number: *OL*

My heart skips a beat. He's on to me. I should've kept moving towards the main gate; I'm stuck in here.

The door swings open. The light. He can probably see the light coming from my screen. I put my phone away again. I can tell by the slow pace it's the killer. This calculated, cocky pace. He is moving towards the seats. He is in the back row, scanning, trying to find me. I try to be as quiet as possible. A shot of anxiety hits me when I realise I haven't turned off the sound on my mobile. I hope the girls don't text me now. Just stay here, Ing, be quiet. It's fairly dark in here, he might not—

The lights are switched on. I feel a bit disorientated, but the moment I centre myself, I can see those god-awful boots. He is standing by the middle row. I know what I'm about to see.

He glares right at me, the deepest glare flowing through that ungodly mask. I try to get back up and make a run for it, but he's too fast. My limp is slowing me down. Before I can even move a step towards the door, he grabs my left hand and stabs it straight onto the wall. I feel the blade cutting right through my nerves. Horrific pain. My hand—it's stuck. As I feel his other hand grabbing my hair, I throw my head backwards and hit him in the face. Another small grunt. He seems momentarily taken aback and steps back a couple of steps. I muster up the courage to break free as I push and slide my hand through the blade until I'm released from the wall. My hand is split into two, my pinky and ring finger hanging loose in the most unnatural way. I'm dizzy, black spots everywhere.

Somehow, I make it out of the cinema room. I just need to get to the fourth floor. Liv and Lu will be there. I drop down again, feeling even weaker than before. The blood from my hand and leg keeps dripping on the wooden floorboards of the hallway. The killer is standing behind me in the hallway. I can't give up. I won't. I try to stand up again, deliriously looking around for any help, but the figure kicks me in my back and pushes the knife down my right arm. He's got me. There's no way out. I wish I could get used to the pain and just push through, but it's starting to become unbearable.

He releases his foot and lets me crawl onto the hallway floor. I keep moving, barely, but I'm not a quitter. The black spots in my eyes are getting bigger. My vision is blurring too. I think I can make it to the staircase. I think I've got this. Pull it together, Ing.

Fourth floor, almost. The killer puts his foot on my back again. He pushes harder and harder. I can't take the pain anymore. I can't move either. I hear a couple of vertebrae cracking. The cracking sounds make me feel defeated. He grabs me from the back and pulls me up. What is he doing? I try to break free from his grip, but there's not enough strength left in my body. He twists my body towards the railing of the staircase.

"Oh, no, no please don't drop me!" I don't know why I am even asking, but I know I won't make it out alive if he pushes me over the bannister from the third floor. As he slowly pushes my body up, he tilts me over the railing. I look down. It's a long way down. I try to find peace in all of this and let go of all the anxiety that is barely keeping me alive. I think I can hear a faint chuckle coming from behind that awful mask. I look around me again to see if anyone's around, but my vision is almost entirely gone. I look up at the killer one more time, trying to focus.

Those eyes; I do know them. I know who this is.

The killer lets go of my body. This is it. I close my eyes and I feel the air blowing through my hair as I fall down. Just let it be over quickly—I can't-

Chapter 19

LUCIJA

The bathroom feels a bit like a temporary safe haven. It's probably Alzy's playlist, together with the company. The little warm blows of Liv's hairdryer touching my cheeks by accident. I love moments like these. The anticipation of a night out, standing next to your besties, gossiping about who'll be there and who won't. All six of us used to cram up against each other, fighting for space in front of the mirrors in order to get ready. Well, except for Alzy, she couldn't care less about makeup. Marieke would usually need a wee in the middle of it, and we all know she's not embarrassed to pull down her trousers and sit down on the toilet right in front of us. A lot of those types of memories have been flooding my mind lately.

"Remember that night you took me to Mont des Arts for the first time, Liv?" I look at her through the bathroom mirror. We're both getting ready for EU night. She looks gorgeous, her wavy dark blonde hair falling over her shoulders and that strapless maroon dress. I have always thought of her as one of those underrated, understated beauties. Very natural looking— flawless skin and the clearest of eyes. She takes her lipstick and carefully applies the dark red shade.

"I think I do. Why did I take you there again? It was mid–September, right?"

"Right. You told me the Art Mountain was your favourite spot in Brussels. Because of the view."

"I remember now. Why are you thinking about that night?"

"It's just one of those moments I'll never forget —being in a new city, a new country, you being so welcoming and showing me all these spots. I remember feeling hopeful. That maybe moving away from Croatia wasn't the worst idea. We were both seated on top of the mountain, if you can call it that, basically a small hill, but still. You were pointing out the National Library on the left with its restaurant rooftop, that lovely symmetrical garden right in front of us, and the old city centre with the town hall behind it. It was the first moment I felt okay in the city, like I had a friend I could rely on."

"You're getting all emotional. You never talk like this." Oliwia stares at me.

"I know, it's just, I should've taken it in more. That spot. I remember that sunset; it was just perfect. The entire sky had this dark orange glow, like a filter almost." I start crying.

"Don't cry, boo. You'll ruin your makeup!"

I can't believe she's just said that. I look at her for a moment. We both burst out laughing. "Who *are* you?" I say in between laughing fits.

"A girl who wants to look good for one night," she replies, still laughing. "I've been looking like absolute shit for days. Oh wow, another one."

I'm not quite sure what she is on about. "Another what?"

"That song! I mean, I knew Czech techno was going to be full-on, but this is next level. I think my eardrums might burst."

We both giggle. "Who *are* we?" I repeat. "Bougie girls listening to hardcore techno in a dorm bathroom. I need a life coach."

"Yes! One of those who brings her own healing crystals and homemade Kombucha to your home, just in case."

"Exactly! Anyway, should we head out? It's 9:34 PM, probably time to get going. We're late!"

"Sure, I think I'm as ready as I'll ever be. By the way, have you texted Ing?"

"No, I wanted to give her some space. Have you?"

"No, hold on—I can see she's been on her phone just a couple of minutes ago, so I guess she'll come over soon too, probably with her roommates. She said she would text us as soon as she was about to head out, so, let's do this."

We both walk out of Liv's dorm room, followed by our silent-as-ever cop. The moment we step outside into the hall, this odd sensation comes rushing over me, as if somebody's watching us. "It's so creepy in here in the evening. Why can't they just leave all the lights on in the hallway?" I ask myself out loud.

"It's a crisis for everyone, even for Europea."

As we make our way up to the fourth floor, Czech folk music floats down the stairs to merrily greet us. I'm not entirely sure why, but I start smiling. A part of me still feels slightly guilty about even going, but something about the uplifting melody draws me in.

"Oh, they've already started the music, Lu—we're really late. Come on!" She grabs my arm and starts running towards the lounge room. The cop seems a bit confused and runs behind us.

"You can stay here," Liv tells the policeman once we arrive at the door. "We'll be fine inside. It's just us girls."

He quickly peeks his head inside the lounge as we enter. I

don't for a second trust that he'll leave us alone inside.

"Alright girls, it seems safe in there. There are no other doors or exits?"

"No, just this one. Thank you, officer."

"I'll be right here if you need me, don't go anywhere else without telling me."

That's it? Good thing I've got Liv with me, cause this cop sure as hell won't save us.

Oliwia and I walk in and close the door behind us. She starts laughing again. "Thank you, officer? Really Lu? Could you sound more sexual?"

I start blushing. "Stop it, I was just being nice for once!"

She pinches my arm and winks at me. We both look at the room and people in front of us. This has always been my favourite room, apart from the actual bedroom dorms. We've always had these amazing nights full of dancing, usually accompanied by some alcohol we somehow managed to smuggle along. The wallpapers have this lovely Art Deco pattern, which makes the place feel a bit like a speakeasy. Ingvild would be proud of me for knowing it's Deco, not Nouveau. The cheap school tables and chairs kind of break the illusion of grandeur, but other than that, the usual chandeliers and Greek columns do give it an air of prestige. The two chaperones, Miss O'deary and Miss Uttväla, are standing next to the snack table, so I guess no special drinks tonight. The music is still playing and there are about twenty girls dancing along to the up-tempo folk songs. They're lost in their own little world, dancing like there's no tomorrow. The retro disco ball and coloured lights hanging from the ceiling add a touch of- I'm not quite sure if I should say flair or tackiness. I didn't actually expect there to be a full-on party here tonight after everything that has happened. Guess I'm wrong; they're really going for it.

The smell of sweat mixed with sweet perfume hits me. Some of these girls could do with a little touch up, Christ. Five or six of them stop for a few seconds and stare at us. It's been like this for a couple of days now. You can tell people just don't know how to act around us anymore. It's usually a mix of pity, fear, awkwardness, or judgement. Two of the girls gently wave hello at us, which feels nice. We both eagerly wave back. I'm trying to read the room, but so far everything feels fine, rather relaxed and upbeat.

"Right. Entering a room definitely does not get any easier, does it?" Liv asks rhetorically. "We need snacks! Come on, the snack table is at the back over there!"

We both run to the end of the lounge. The table is filled with Czech food and drinks. There's a mix of soft cheeses, vegetables, nuts, and meat. The pink lemonade looks really nice, actually.

"Could you grab me a plate, Lu?"

"Sure, hold on."

"You're kidding me!" She slaps my left wrist.

"What? What did I do?"

"No, look!" She points towards the middle of the makeshift dance floor. It's Oliwia's ex, Karla.

"Why are you so surprised it's her? She does live here."

"It's just, she usually never shows up for EU night. I feel like I haven't seen her in weeks."

"So? Go talk to her!"

"Why would I? Nothing's changed." She replies hesitatingly. I hold both of her arms and look deep into her eyes.

"Everything's changed."

Chapter 20

OLIWIA

I can't believe I'm about to do this. My palms are already sweaty. I haven't talked to her in months. Maybe she doesn't even want to talk to me. I mean, look at her, dancing underneath those purple spotlights. She looks so ethereal. That long, light brown hair, those light green eyes, those high cheekbones. I can't get over how beautiful she is. I don't think I ever did get over her.

Before I can muster up the courage to step towards her, she notices me in the middle of her fairy dance and smiles at me.

"Livvy!" She continues dancing and starts elegantly moving towards me. She grabs my hands, and we both dance. The rest of the world slips away for a moment. It's just green eyes, light brown hair, and smiles. Escapism has never felt so good. I've missed her energy. Let's just be honest here, I've missed *her*, full stop.

After what seems like forever in the best way possible, the song stops. We both stand there, a bit out of breath, looking at each other, holding hands, smiling.

"So," she starts, as brave as ever, "been a while since we danced together."

"It has." I look down at the mosaic tiles. Why does she always make me feel so nervous? I try to dry my hands by rubbing them on my dress. Classy, Liv—ever the lady.

"I haven't seen you in ages. The movie club isn't the same without you, you know? A lot isn't. Listen, Livvy, I won't ask how you're doing. Not because I don't care, but because I know you've been asked a thousand times lately."

"Thank you, Karla. I appreciate that." Her talking to me the way she always used to gives me a warm, safe feeling inside.

"But unless you've changed, I am guessing you could use some liquid courage tonight."

"What? Where? How did you slip that in with the teachers lurking around?"

"Try the yellow punch on the left side of the table. Thank me later." She grins at me, her eyes sparkling.

We both walk towards the snack table and take some punch. I see Lucija standing by herself at the other side of the table. I signal for her to come over, feeling bad about leaving her by herself. She looks a bit lost. She walks towards Karla first and gives her a kiss on the left cheek.

"Hey, Karla, it's been a hot second!" I'm grateful she's nice to her. Lord knows I vented way too much to Lucija when I ended things with her.

"It has been, indeed. Have some punch!" She passes a glass to Lucija.

"No thanks. I'm not really a punch kind of gal."

"Oh, you most definitely will be after trying *this* punch." She winks and pushes the glass in Lucija's hands. She takes a careful sip.

"Woah, that's some serious punch! Who has spiked it?"

"Yours truly." Karla smiles at Lucija and looks back at me.

118

There's something about that smile. So genuine, so open, it would melt the toughest of hearts.

"Lucija, would you mind if I talked to Oliwia for a moment? I need to tell her something."

"Sure, absolutely, I'll just awkwardly dance amongst semi strangers, no biggie." Lucija winks at me, signalling an enthusiastic thumbs up and walks towards the dance floor on her own.

Stay calm, Liv, stay calm. What does she need to tell me?

Karla takes my right hand and pulls me towards the chairs next to the snack table. We sit down and remain silent for a moment. It brings me back to when we'd just sit in the clearing of the forest near Jette. She'd bring one of her movie review magazines and I'd just sit there in silence next to her, on our little rock. Trying not to be too obvious about looking at her all the time. I was never nervous about having to fill the silence, it felt just right. I was home.

Lucija's dance moves make me chuckle a bit, as gracious as she is, dancing is not her forte.

"So, what is it you wanted to tell me?" I rub my left thumb over my ring finger, trying to find comfort in my grandmother's ring.

"I've been meaning to talk to you. For some days, but, well, I didn't know how or when to approach you."

"Okay. I mean, I get it. Most people have been acting super weird around us; it's not just you."

"No, that's not what I mean. Obviously, you can talk to me about your friends and what's going on, but this is about me."

"About you? What do you mean?"

"I don't know if you even want to hear this, but—I came out."

I feel shocked. "You did? You—I mean, to who?"

119

"Everyone. Literally, everyone knows."

"So literally everyone includes—?"

"My parents? Yeah. And guess what? They didn't actually kick me out. They were fairly cool about it."

"Are you for real?" I jump up and hug her. "This is massive news, Karla! I know how scared you were of their reaction! No way. This is such good news, the best I've heard in ages!"

I look into her eyes. I really want to kiss her, but I stop myself. "So why didn't you tell me before?"

"I mean, this all happened like five days ago. I wanted to give you some space and just let you be with your friends after—you know?"

"I know." I look down again, scared of what I'm about to ask her. "So what does that mean?"

"Me coming out?"

"Yes. What does that mean - for us?"

"It means things are different now, Liv. It means, I'm still here. I still care about you. I mean, I don't want to throw any extra emotional mess in your face, but I'm here. And this time, if you'd allow me to, I could be all in. I will be." She sounds confident, but I know she is just as nervous as I am.

"I—I still care about you too. This is all a lot to comprehend and take in, to be honest. I've been wanting to hear you say those words since we first started dating. I don't want to rush into things, but- life has changed so much in so little time. I don't want to waste any of it wondering what might have been. I could be all in too. I will be too."

We look at each other. There it is again: the entire world disappears when I look into those eyes. I run my hands through her hair. She touches my left cheek. Electricity surges through my entire body. I am never normally the one who makes a move, but tonight is different. I kiss her. She kisses me back, a slow and gentle peck at first, which organically turns into the passionate type of kiss I needed more than I'd realised. Her tongue caresses mine, we lose ourselves in the moment. I've missed her, I've missed those soft, full lips of hers. At the same time, it feels like she's always been here. It's like having this safe, yet exciting comfort blanket back in my life. I didn't expect Czechia to bring such a twist tonight. But I'm glad it did; I needed a win. I needed something to fight for. Someone.

I snap out of the moment as I feel my phone vibrating. "Sorry, do you mind if I check it, Karla? It's probably Ingvild."

"Of course not, take it." She smiles at me gently, stroking my back.

I quickly grab my phone. One new message. Not this. Not now please.

Unknown Number: *L*

Chapter 21

LUCIJA

I can tell something's up. Oliwia is running towards me. She looks panicked. Some of the girls can sense the tension in the room and stare at both of us.

"Liv, what is it? You look so pale!"

"I received a message from—it says L." She stares at me, eyes full of pain and fear.

"L?" It sinks in. That's not just Oliwia's letter missing, but Ingvild's too.

"Oh God, Lu, do you know what that means? Ingvild! The killer got to Ingvild!"

"Calm down. We can't be sure that actually happened!" I'm not sure who I'm trying to convince, Liv or myself.

"Then where the hell is she?" Oliwia starts speaking more loudly. The other girls in the lounge are slowly stepping away from the two of us. Karla is standing right behind Oliwia, but she keeps her distance too.

"Liv, let's just stay here. The cops are out there. Let's just call LeBeaux and—"

"I'm next. You know that, right? I'm next. You're the Final

Girl; you're L."

Oliwia starts hyperventilating. She touches her chest with her left hand. Karla walks up to her carefully.

"Liv, are you okay? What's happening?"

"Give her some space, Karla. She's just received a text."

"A text, from who?"

I look sternly into her eyes. "The killer. Please give us a moment." I am aware of how protective I am being over Liv right now, but frankly, I don't care.

I hear some gasps and whispers around me from the other girls the moment I say the word "killer."

"Liv, come on, let's walk to the policeman. He can help us!" I take her hand and walk towards the door of the lounge. Karla tries to say something, but instead she kindly pets Oliwia on the back as we make a move for it. The other girls stare at us, eyes full of shock and mistrust. We walk past the dance floor, past the group of scared girls towards the door.

As I swing the door open, the policeman falls down onto the ground. Dead. Headless. The killer is standing right in front of me.

Chapter 22

OLIWIA

So this is what the killer's mask looks like. Actually, seeing this figure standing in front of me after hearing so much about it is not what I expected. I thought I'd be prepared, ready to tackle the person who killed my best friends, but as I come face-to-face with the killer, my heart sinks. I can hear the screaming of the girls behind us. I scan the room, searching for something sharp—how didn't I think of this before? I should've known better as the film geek—but can't find anything. All this talk about slashers and tropes, but I still forgot to actually protect myself and my friends. I could kick myself. In the flash of a second, Lucija grabs one of the plastic school chairs next to her and smashes it hard into the killer's face. More screams.

"Livvy, be careful!" I look back and can tell Karla looks petrified. I run back to her and grab her left hand with both of mine. "I am careful. I'm ready to fight this bastard." A white lie never killed anybody. Well, maybe this time.

The killer loses his balance from the hit and falls forward onto the ground. I look at the other girls in the lounge and shout, "Get out of here, all of you! Run to the entrance and call for the guards. Tell them the killer's here!"

A handful of girls shoot past us towards the entrance of our boarding school. The chaperones are the first to flee. Thanks for saving us, adults. The rest hesitatingly start following. The only time I've ever heard this much collective chaotic yelping was when the women on *The Bachelor* were fighting over their future husband for one-on-one time.

The figure stands back up. There is something about the way that he gets back up that makes him look even taller and ominous than last time, as if this temporary setback only made him more determined and ready to end us. His shoulders look stronger, his stance wider. He's got both fists clenched tightly, one of them holding a giant butcher's knife.

I look at Lucija. What should we do? There are about six or seven girls left in the room.

"Get out!" I yell, but the figure moves towards the girls and plunges the knife into one of the girls' stomachs. I think it's Ricka, but I'm not sure. She lets out a harrowing sound, as he pulls out the knife again and stabs it into another girl's stomach right next to Ricka. I hold onto Karla's hand even tighter and try to comfort her. Lu's standing next to us as well now. The three of us are staring at the mayhem unfolding in front of us. Frozen with terror. The killer has lost it, completely lost it. This unwavering rage—it's as if Lu hitting him turned his rage button up to a hundred.

I look back at Karla, panicking more than I'd like to admit, "Karla, get out, now! I don't want you to—" My voice cracks.

"I don't want to leave you, Liv." She's got tears in her eyes.

We all look behind us as the killer slashes into yet another girl. He's killed three girls already. He's like a steamroller rolling over everyone in a matter of seconds. I block out my emotions consciously; otherwise, I'll lose it.

"I'm asking you, leave! Lucija and I have to go find Ingvild. We can't leave her behind!" Lucija looks back at me. She is shocked by the sight of the bloodbath unravelling in front of us.

"You were totally right Liv," she whispers. "Act Three."

"Lucija, listen, we need to find Ingvild; she might still be alive!" I hear more shouting as the killer works his way through the group of girls left behind.

Lu sees that Karla is still holding onto me.

"Karla, I'm sorry, but you need to go, now! Liv and I need to look for Ingvild. You need to call for help!"

Karla looks slightly annoyed at Lucija. "No, I'm not leaving her. I can protect her, I can protect you too."

The killer looks back at our little quarrel. It seems as if he is about to walk towards us. Lucija pushes Karla out the door. She looks completely puzzled.

"Get out, get help!"

Karla wants to run back, but is swallowed up by the remaining group of girls fleeing towards the exit. The other girls drag Karla with her to the main gate of the halls.

I'm in shock. "Why did you do that?"

"Because I know you don't want to lose her again. I'm sorry, this is your best bet. She's safe out there."

As angry as I am, I get it. No time to discuss. I hope I'll see her again. The thought of it scares the life out of me, so I snap out of it again. I need to make it out alive, even more so now than before. I *need* to see Karla again. I clench my fists too, just like the killer. I'm not giving up that easily. Lucija and I look at each other. We both nod, time to look for Ingvild.

The killer is still slashing his way through our dorm mates —I look at the floor for a second, a bunch of bodies on top of each other, blood everywhere. It's too horrible to fathom. His back is turned towards us, so we decide to run out.

Lucija takes my hand and, we start running down the hallway on the fourth floor. We flow through the hallway as a team, ready for battle. We look at each other knowingly. This is the night everything is going to unravel. As we go past the staircase, I notice blood drops on the railing. I don't want to give into the fear, but something tells me they could be Ingvild's.

"Lu, look—blood!"

She tilts her head slowly. "Oh God, I hope it's not—"

"Don't say it! Don't! We'll find her, let's go to her dorm room. It's room 214, right?"

"Right, yes, I think so." We continue running. The killer seems to still be in the lounge as we hear the echoes of at least two girls yelling for help.

As we make it down to the second floor, we hear someone walking down the spiral case. No more shouting in the lounge room. I know what that means. We nod at each other, as determined as we've ever been; time to speed up. I see the room tag with 214 on it and drag Lucija even faster. We almost stumble over our feet.

Lucija swings open Ingvild's door and screams loudly. I put my hands over her mouth. "Lu, shhh, quiet! What is it?" I look inside the room and notice the three bloodied beds. It's as if I am becoming numb to these sights. It's just too much to process in one night.

"Close the door, Lu! And from now on, whispers only."

She quietly shuts the door. We both stand there, looking at Ingvild's bed, slightly out of breath. I can feel the sweat drops trickling down my back into my dress.

"Does that mean"—Lu looks at me with some hope in her eyes—"that she made it out alive? Her bed—look, there's no blood."

"Maybe—she's tough. Where would she have gone?"

"Check your phone. Has she texted or called you?"

"No, nothing, just that text saying 'L.' How about you?"

Lucija takes out her phone and looks right at me. "I have three missed calls."

"Is it her? Is it Ingvild?"

Lucija looks at her screen and seems confused.

"Lu! Who was it?"

"LeBeaux. The detective has called me three times." We both sigh, disappointed it wasn't Ingvild.

"Well, call her back!"

"Okay, okay, hold on."

"Don't put her on speaker this time; the killer might hear you. Make sure you whisper. I'll put my ear next to yours so I can hear her too."

"Right."

LeBeaux picks up almost immediately again. "Lucija, is that you?"

"Yes, I have to whisper; the killer is here. He has killed some girls in our lounge. One of the policemen is decapitated too."

"Was it Jim?" LeBeaux sounds shocked.

We both look at each other awkwardly. "Eh, I don't know. I didn't see his head."

"Oh, that's awful. The reason I tried calling you is because we know who the killer is." Lucija opens her eyes widely. My hand palms are becoming sweaty, again.

"Who is it?" Lu asks quietly.

"It's Matej. I wanted to call you because I have proof he has

128

entered the boarding school."

"So, it's been him all along? My boyfriend?" Lu asks. She doesn't sound convinced.

"I'm on my way to Europea Halls. I'll be there in about fifteen minutes, Lucija. Hang on! Where can I find you?"

"We're in Ingvild's dorm room, room 214, looking for her, but we haven't found her yet."

"She's gone missing? I told you all to stay together! Okay, stay there! Stay together!" LeBeaux hangs up the phone.

We still haven't heard any sounds in the hallway. I guess everyone has left. No idea where the guards are either.

"So, what's next?" Lu asks. "She hasn't called us and no texts. Where do you think she would've run to? Should we check the entrance? The gardens?"

"I'm not sure. I hope she's made it out in time. If we go to the entrance, we're safe, but she could still be stuck inside, you know?"

"Or we just wait here until LeBeaux comes, and we look for her together?"

"No, we need to do something. Maybe she's been stabbed, or maybe she's waiting for us somewhere. We can't leave her behind, Lu!"

"Agreed! Okay, how about we–"

"Wait, boo, I got another text." My hands are shaking. My phone almost drops out of my sweaty, shaky hands.

"What does it say? Who is it?"

Karel: *Meet me in the library, seventh floor. I can explain everything.*

Chapter 23

LUCIJA

"Why would Karel text you? I'm the one he talked to after music class." I'm slightly annoyed by this.

"No idea, he hasn't texted me in months. I bet it's about Matej. Those two used to be friends, right?"

"He told me they were good again. I guess you're onto something. He probably knows where Matej was hanging out."

"Or what if it's a trap?" Oliwia has her detective/slasher knowledge goggles on. "What if he's luring us up there 'cause he knows there won't be anyone else there at this time of day?"

"Karel? Do you think he has anything to do with all of this? That dude's so random. He's never even really been part of our friend circle."

"I have no idea. But this time I want to be prepared."

"What do you mean?"

"When the killer stood in front of us, we had nothing! No pepper spray, no knives, nothing. If we want to be smart about this, we need to go to the kitchen and get us some knives."

To be honest, in the midst of all this chaos, I hadn't even thought about that. Good thing I've got Liv in my life. I have heard about fight or flight; seems like her fight mode is on. I'm wavering between both.

"You want to go to the kitchen? But Liv, that's on the first floor. And from there we have to go to the seventh floor. That's a lot of opportunities for the killer to hear or find us."

We both think for a while. In the meantime, there's still not a sound in the hallway. What if the killer is just waiting for us somewhere?

I have an idea. "I've got it! We can take the staff's lift from the kitchen directly to the library! It's normally off limits, but I don't think there's any security or anything. We've just been too chicken to actually ever use it."

"The lift? Oh right, the elevator!"

"Lift, elevator. Whatever." We both smile for a second. We've had these chats about which version of English all of us speak. Some of us were taught American English at school, whereas others were taught UK English (I suppose it's called the Queen's English or something? Or is it the King's English now?). We all ended up agreeing we speak a bit of a mix. Our English teacher told us once at Europea that we basically speak European English, which is usually influenced by all types of versions of English. Anyway, where was I? Oh right, getting knives to stab the killer. Guess my mind needed a little break from all the killings. "Let's go then. If we quietly open the door, we can just walk to the first floor. I think if we run, we'll make too much noise."

"A hundred percent. Let's do this!" She seems determined, but there's a sadness in her eyes too.

"Hey, Liv, we'll find Ing, okay?"

"Okay, thanks, we will." I hug her tightly, because I can tell we are both fearing the same fate for Ingvild. She hasn't been online since the last time we checked. I noticed, but I didn't have the heart to tell Oliwia.

I gently open the door and look both left and right. Not a sound nor person around us. Shouldn't the guards be here by now? Did none of the girls who ran out warn them? We both walk towards the staircase as silently as we can. It doesn't help that the flooring is made of old oak boards. We try to almost glide across the boards like a pair of ballet dancers tiptoeing towards our morbid destination. We're almost at the staircase when one of the boards creaks loudly. I panic and look at Liv.

"Just keep going," she whispers. "It's fine. Go, go!"

We head down the stairs to the first floor, faster than before. We stand still for a moment and look around us. Nothing. The only thing I hear is the faint buzzing of the lights in the lounge above us and some cars passing by in the distance. This entire building seems empty apart from us and the killer.

I continue and speed up the pace a bit more. The kitchen is situated to the left at the end of the hall. When we are halfway across the hall, I hear a loud thud above us. I'm not sure if it's on the second or third floor, but we instantly know we should start running. Flight mode kicks in. We run as fast as we can to the kitchen door and quietly close it behind us. As we look around, we see some white, worn kitchen cabinets that we use to barricade the entrance. I haven't been here in ages. Normally we are not really allowed in here anyway, because the kitchen staff prepares all our meals, but sometimes a girl needs a midnight snack. Oliwia instinctively yanks a large butcher's knife from the kitchen island and passes it to me.

"Here, take it."

I hesitate for a second.

"What am I supposed to do with this?"

"I don't know! Defend, fight, stab, whatever you have to do to stay alive!"

I firmly nod my head and take the knife. She takes another knife for herself and looks back at me.

"Are we ready for this?"

"I'm not sure I'm ready for anything at this point. What do you mean?"

"The library! Let's go find Karel and see what he has to say for himself. Where's that lift, elevator, whatever thingy?"

"It's at the back there, next to the freezers!"

A loud banging noise jolts us out of our plans. We both lose our cool for a second and scream loudly. Liv grabs my left hand tightly. The killer is violently banging on the door, trying to get in. There's a sense of urgency to his continuous banging. It seems like from the moment the killing frenzy started in the lounge room, something has snapped for the killer. He's no longer calm and collected, but rather chaotic and full of rage. The cabinets are blocking him from coming in, but for how long?

"Follow me. Run!" We both head towards the left and press the up button. The lift starts moving, but it is coming from the seventh floor. Why would it come from the library? Karel might have taken the lift too, but I'm not sure how he would even know about it. He's never been in these halls as far as I'm aware, except maybe for a hookup. Word gets around quickly in these halls, and his reputation isn't exactly the best.

The killer frantically and repeatedly stabs through the wooden door. We both scream again. The barricade falls down to the ground. We both notice the figure is messing with the lock. We lock eyes again. I can tell Liv is just as scared as I am, but somehow there's no time to think clearly. Everything is moving too fast. I squeeze her hand.

133

The lift door opens with a loud clicking sound. It's one of those old, shabby service lifts that looks like old aluminum wrapping paper. Not sure how strong this thing is, but it'll have to do.

We both rush in and press button 7. The moment the door closes and we move up, we can hear a loud cracking noise below us. The killer has opened the kitchen door. We stand there for a second, still hand in hand, looking at the lift buttons lighting up from 2 to 3.

"That was a close one," Liv says. "I can't even imagine." She straightens her back and composes herself again. "Right, Lucija, be prepared."

"For what though?"

"Maybe Karel is with Ingvild, hiding in the library, I'm not sure, but we can't trust him."

We stand in silence again, waiting for the lights around the buttons to move up from 3 to 4. The lift feels quite shaky. I'm not sure this was the best idea. Liv squeezes my hand a little tighter. "We've got this. We've got each other." She continues staring at the buttons in front of us. I do the same. The light goes from 5 to 6. My body starts rocking back and forth gently, as if it's preparing me for what's to come.

The light at floor 7 lights up. We arrive at the library. I semi-expect someone to jump out on us, but as the door opens, all I see is the massive, dark library floor in front of me. There's not a single sound.

Chapter 24

OLIWIA

I haven't been in here in—well, no idea how long. As I look around, the first thing I notice are the wooden ladders and the tiny, bronze spiral cases on each end of the room. The first time I stepped foot in the library, it reminded me of Belle's library in *Beauty and the Beast*. I guess it must be those moveable ladders. The ceilings are made of massive dark wood. I think Ingvild mentioned to me once that the library was inspired by a university in Dublin, but I'm not sure now. In front of us we see the main hall of the library with tons of bookshelves—I can smell the dust on them immediately as we enter—at the back and the white, leather couches all over the hallway, placed in cosy positions with tons of dark green book lights around it. The stained-glass windows all around are stunning as well. They remind me of those Gothic churches you've got all around Flanders in the north of Belgium. The moonlight shines through them quite proudly, projecting bits of red and dark blue across the entire room. I had always thought of the seventh floor as romantic and exciting, but this is the first time it scares the living daylights out of me. It's not exactly pitch black in here;

we can still make out shapes and shades thanks to those stained-glass windows, but we instinctively know not to turn on the lights.

Last time I came here was for a much more romantic purpose. Karla and I did come in here a couple of times—what can I say? Aisle L is known as "Lover's Lane" for a reason. The absence of sound terrifies me. Karel should be here.

I hold the knife in my left hand a little tighter. It calms me down for a moment.

I'm not sure where we should go or if we should call out for Karel. The enormity of both the room and the night falls heavy on my shoulders. This is the top floor. It feels like we're reaching some sort of ending. The final stop on the lift. I'm just scared to death that the ending is, well, to put it not-so-eloquently, our deaths.

Lucija signals me to start walking down the aisles on the right side in search for Karel, so I follow her. As we walk around, I keep looking everywhere for any sign of life, any sign of Ingvild. Maybe they're both here waiting for us. I'm scared that the killer will pop up at any given second. Each aisle is covered with books, shadows, and dread. The further along we go, the more scared I become. Something feels off here. This all feels like a set-up, and I'm afraid we've walked right into it.

We hear a faint tapping sound two aisles ahead. I jump up, and so does Lu. I'm not sure how much sweat one human can produce, but my glands are being tested tonight.

Lucija nods at me knowingly and we both follow the tapping sounds. I stop her and whisper, "Are we sure about this?"

She looks at me confused. "I mean, no, but what else can we do?"

"Look, if he ends up being the killer, we go for the head—

deal?"

"The head?"

"In slashers, all these dumb blondes always aim for the stomach, but we need to aim for the head. Or the throat; that's good too."

Lucija stands there, a bit shocked. "I don't know if I'm ready to stab someone in the—you know, there." She can't say it.

"We've got this, you and I. We're in this together, okay?"

"Okay, we've got this." I can tell she is amping herself up.

"We've got this." She repeats, more to herself this time. She jumps up and down a bit, readying herself for the next move.

We both walk towards aisle L. Of course, it's the only aisle any of us knows about in the library, I guess.

As we walk past aisle H, we can already see a figure sitting down in the next aisle. This is it. Who's it going to be? It feels like I am walking in quicksand. With each and every step, the effort to keep moving grows. My legs feel heavy, my knees weak. I want to reach aisle L, but I'm also dreading what or who will be waiting for us there.

Lucija screams sharply and holds up her knife in front of her. "You??" I rush after Lucija to see who she is talking about.

It's him, Matej. He jolts up and holds up his right hand in front of him. "Wait! Wait! Oliwia, are you there?"

I am standing behind Lucija now.

"I—I'm here. What do you want from me?" It feels like he is part of the trap. He doesn't look very menacing—more like terrified. I keep my guard up though. Twists are part of the final act.

"This isn't about Lucija; this is about you, Oliwia." He looks at me, scared.

Lucija replies quickly, "What is that supposed to mean? I'm

next? LeBeaux called us and said you—you're the killer." She looks at him with what comes across as a mix of confusion, fear, and love. Broken love, but it's still there. There's no denying it.

"What?" Matej shouts out loud. "Me? No, look, I needed to run away. People thought it was me, but I was trying to warn everyone."

"Warn everyone about what?" I ask.

That moment the lift door opens, and we hear calm, collected footsteps down the main hall of the library. Lucija and I look at each other again. We're both holding up our knives towards Matej.

I whisper at her, "Lucija, what if he's right? If he isn't the killer, then who is walking into the reading room?"

If the killer is walking down the library as we speak, it appears that he has calmed down again. The pace of the footsteps has gone back to ominous and calculated.

Matej replies quickly. "Let me explain, please. Just let me explain!"

Lucija looks at me nervously. "I don't know about this, Oliwia. Maybe we should run?"

"Run where? We're on the top floor. Okay Matej, explain what? Where's Karel?"

"He asked me to come here. To the library, he showed me on an old map how to get here."

"But how did you get past the guards?"

"They—they weren't there when I entered."

Lucija scoffs. "Right, where were they, then? Taking a power nap in the lounge? You have a lot of explaining to do! Why were you even at Alzy's? Were you two hooking up? Be honest!" Her eyes are open wide, full of rage. "I've got a knife in my hands, Matej, tell me the truth!"

For a moment I had forgotten about the footsteps in the reading room, I got too sucked into the drama unfolding in front of me.

"Guys, wait!" I implore them to be quiet. "Wait, what happened to the footsteps? Listen!" All three of us stop talking and try to hear any sounds around us. Nothing, as if the figure has vanished, just like that.

"Where did they go?" I ask quietly.

I've never been one for too much silence, but this time, the silence feels deadlier than ever. As the three of us stand there, I can tell Matej is just as scared as Lucija and me. There's no way he's the killer. It could be Karel though. He seems to have lured us all up here.

A dark figure jumps behind Matej and stabs him in the middle of his back. Matej lets out a blood-curdling sound. The killer came out of nowhere. Matej stiffens up and his eyes start rolling upwards. We all stand there in complete shock.

"Matej!" Lucija screams out and runs towards him and the killer.

"Stab him, Lu! stab the killer!" Matej begs her. His entire body starts shaking as the killer starts lifting him, using the blade as leverage. Matej starts shaking even more, his entire body in tremors. Lucija looks at me, confused. I run towards Matej as well and signal Lucija to do it.

Matej looks at Lucija and starts speaking in a slurred way: "Lucija, I had to make sure—Lu, you—"

Before we get a proper chance to stab the killer, he pulls out the knife from Matej's back, so Matej drops down to the ground. The killer quickly disappears back into the dark library.

Lu and I both jump back for a second as Matej's bloodied body flops down right in front of us. The smacking sound as his body

139

hits the floor is truly horrific.

Lucija drops down next to Matej and starts sobbing.

"Matej? Matej, stay with me." I try to pull her away from him, as I can tell Matej is already gone, but she won't budge.

"Lucija, come on, we need to go!" I scan the aisle again, but I can't see where the killer ran off to.

"Lu, the killer's still here, come on. Matej is dead. I'm sorry, but he's gone."

Lucija looks completely deflated. I try to pull her up, but she is working against me. "Leave me alone! I should've trusted him! I was such a shitty girlfriend. How could I think he was the killer?"

"It's not your fault. We all thought he was at some point. Come on, we need to run! Please, Lu, don't give up now!"

I feel someone forcefully grabbing my hair. I am being pulled back. I flop down to the ground and start screaming. The pressure on my scalp is almost unbearable. As I lay there on the ground, I can see the killer looking down at me with that creepy mask, tilting his head, as if waiting for the next part of his wretched little game.

"Lu, help! Help!" The figure continues to pull my hair and drag me down the aisles, moving rather swiftly towards the reading room. I try to claw at him and kick my legs up, but the figure is stronger than me. I stupidly dropped the knife out of shock when he grabbed me, so I feel defenceless. Guess I'm not the best at defending myself; I've learned that the hard way this night.

"Lu, where are you? Help!" My head is pounding. "Leave me alone, you freak! Let go of me! Help!" I guess I saw it coming when I received that message saying "L." I don't want to die though. As I am being pulled into the reading room, all I can think of is Karla. She is waiting for me at the main gates. I can't give up on this, I can't give up on us.

The dragging stops. I'm trying to understand what the killer wants. I look up to the massive gilded ceiling, full of golden angels and saints. The beauty of it feels overpoweringly terrifying.

I feel the killer's hands around my waist as he pulls me up and drops me down on one of the white leather sofas. He lets go.

I sit there, on my own on the sofa, the killer in front of me. I'm looking at the killer's hands, waiting for him to pull out his knife. It doesn't happen. The figure just stands there, looking down at me, barely moving. There's that tilt again, that menacing move.

A part of me wants to make a run for it towards the elevator, but a bigger part of me is too curious to find out why he is just standing there. Is this what Matej was trying to tell me?

"What— what do you want? Why are you doing this?"

Then it hits me. I know who this is. Of course.

I can see a tiny strand of blonde hair behind the mask. But it's not the hair that made me realise, it's the eyes.

As she removes the mask slowly, I look LeBeaux in the eyes.

"Piercing eyes," I say. "You."

"Me," LeBeaux replies, a dark smirk on her face. "Yes, darling, me." I try to jump up, but those strong yet elegant hands of hers push me down onto the sofa again instantly. "No need to run; it's pointless. I've been training for this for years. I've outrun Ingvild too."

"What did you do to her?"

"Well, you did spot the drops of blood in the hallway, didn't you? I heard you. She had a nasty little fall."

I want to yell and scream at her, but what comes out are tears. Tears of frustration, anger, sadness, powerlessness. In a way there's some relief there too. Finally, I know who's been behind all of this. I can put a face to who has killed my friends. LeBeaux looks at me and starts smiling. Out of nowhere, I can see a figure walking behind her, walking towards me, holding up a knife.

It's Lucija. She signals me to look away. I decide to distract her, entertain her even. "Why would you kill all of our friends?"

"Why? Does Miss Thang need a motive?" She's feeling almighty, I can tell. This is what she wanted, to toy with me, to play with all of us.

"We're good people, all of us! None of us deserved to die so young!"

"Good people? Really? Rich spoiled, bratty bitches is what you are. All of you. I know you Europea kids. Always feeling better than the rest of us. I had to work for where I got in life."

"You had to work to become a killer? Good on you." It almost feels good to tell her off, but I am still terrified of the repercussions.

She jumps forward. "Don't you test me! You'll never know what it feels like, growing up in complete poverty, working for people like you who are so entitled, they have no clue about the real world out there."

"So you're just jealous? That's your motive, really? You want money?" I put on my bravest face, but inside I am trembling with fear.

"Money? All I want is—" she spins around quickly. "Hey, Lucija."

Lucija jolts up.

"Did you think I didn't notice you in those mirrors there behind you?" She grabs Lucija by her shoulders and throws her on the sofa next to me.

Lucija quickly grabs my hand and stares at LeBeaux. Her entire body is tense.

"Your turn," LeBeaux says slowly to Lucija.

"No, don't hurt her!" I shout.

"No, dear. I won't."

Lucija pulls out her knife, looks at me, and stabs me in the stomach.

"*She* will."

I sit there, dumbfounded, still holding onto Lu's hand. "Lu?" I say, as I touch my bloodied stomach.

Chapter 25

LUCIJA

Surprise. I know, I know, some of you readers will claim you knew it was me all along. Some of you found out halfway through. But let's be honest here; most of you didn't know. I could've told you from the beginning, but that'd be so lame, right? Marieke did say in the beginning my meeting with LeBeaux was taking so long, remember? I mean, it was the perfect opportunity for her and me to go over the details. I've thrown in little clues here and there throughout the book, but I guess you'll have to go back and find them.

It was actually kind of fun, befriending people you want to kill. I couldn't do it myself; it would've been too basic, too transparent. But LeBeaux, that woman is the real deal. I found her on the internet, the dark webs I believe noobs call it. She had been training to become a real killer for years. She might claim she doesn't have a motive, but just wait until you find out. She just needed a push. She needed me, basically.

When we first started chatting, I was still living in Split. My parents started getting worried about me when I killed our dog. That whiny little bastard had it coming. It awoke something in me I didn't even know I had—true courage, true strength. They say the first kill is followed by the awakening phase. I didn't really get a chance to go further, 'cause I was monitored by those two goddamn assholes twenty-four seven. When they brought in the school psychologist, it was the final straw. I needed to get out of there. So I pretended, which as you know by now I am pretty good at. I pretended it was a psychotic attack, a moment of mania, but that I was *so sorry* for what I had done, I just needed a clean slate. A new beginning. That's where Daddy's embassy connections came in handy. I'm fairly sure they couldn't wait to get rid of me and put me in a boarding school far away from Croatia. I mean, everyone in Split knew who I was all of a sudden, and my parents hated that I had smothered their spotless reputation. That is, until they got divorced. They couldn't handle me, always shouting about what the "right move" would be for me. According to Mom, it was Brussels. According to Dad, it was an institution, a mental ward if you will. After the divorce, Mom came with me to Brussels, not 'cause she cared, but because she was scared of what I am capable of, I think. She wanted to make sure I had really changed. Surprise, Mom!

And why these girls, you may ask. They were just so easy to fool. They were all so obsessed with themselves and the way they curated their own lives that they never really took an interest in who I am or what had happened to me. The perfect bait.

MIOLAA isn't just about who's next in the list; it is a countdown to me, Lucija, your perfect Final Killer.

Chapter 26

OLIWIA

"You didn't twist the knife." LeBeaux looks at Lucija, she seems disappointed.

"Oh right, sorry!" she replies and quickly twists the knife in my stomach. The blade cuts through my stomach and I hear something being crushed. They both calmly smile.

"So, how does it feel, Lucija? This is your first, right?"

Lucija stares at the knife and the blood. "It is. It feels intense, like I've got all this power."

I stare at Lucija. "You? Why?" I feel an intense pain in my stomach, but I try to stay calm and focused.

LeBeaux starts laughing. "This girl really loves a good motive. Do you want to tell her, Lucija? Or should I?"

"There's not much to tell, Liv. LeBeaux and I have been working together for a while."

"Did you—did you do any of the killings?"

"No, not until now. It's finally my turn. We wanted to keep the BFF for last. I couldn't have done this without our dear detective here, by the way. She's got all the connections too, right?" She winks at LeBeaux, who eagerly replies.

"Right! I mean, cloning phone numbers isn't exactly rocket science. I was the one who sent you the message from Karel, and that unknown number? Lucija's dad's phone, well, cloned. So there, it all traces back to him. When all of this is over, Daddy can go to jail."

I think for a second, trying to keep up. "What about the policemen and the guards?"

"Oh, I rang up the police office and told everyone we had caught the killer. They all left; there's no one here, girl. I told them Jim and Jeff helped me out, but the entire corps is too lazy to actually verify my words. Apparently, they genuinely trust me. I'm sure they're all waiting for me at the station, ready to crack open a bottle of champagne. And those guards were useless at defending themselves. Those poor bastards didn't see it coming. Oh, and another thing. In our version Matej was working together with Lucija's father."

"Why would those two work together? They don't even know each other. What's the real reason behind all of this?"

"This is getting exhausting, all these questions! Have you not seen what happens when I am triggered? I mean, hello, lounge room? I was talking here! Lucija, can you shut her up for a second?" I'm afraid of what that means. I stare at Lucija, still in complete disbelief.

"Sure!" Lucija perks up as LeBeaux smiles at her. She grabs the knife and stabs me again in the same spot. The pain intensifies. I don't know how much longer I can cope. I lower my head and start sobbing. I'm not sure whether it's this biting pain or the realisation of Lu's betrayal that sets me off. I can hear Lucija laughing hysterically.

"Can't believe I haven't done this before! And I'm so glad I get to do it with you, Liv! Why are you crying? You're the Final

Girl. That's what you wanted, right? To be the heroine of the story." She glares at me, genuinely curious about my answer.

LeBeaux interrupts. "Except in this story, the Final Girl doesn't make it out alive. Her bestie and the clever detective do."

"I've always treated you right!" I whisper. "All of us did. We welcomed you with arms wide open. How could you? Don't you feel guilty?" A hint of anger sets in.

"Guilt? No, I've never felt that one. Must be a bitch feeling, guilt. And welcoming, really? You took me in as some sort of toy, a cheap little Croatian project you thought you could all mould into your Europea Bohemian Bourgeois crap. None of you even asked me about my past."

"Because we respected you, we didn't want to push you, we—" Another sharp pain hits my stomach. I am out of breath for a moment. I'm starting to feel lightheaded.

I lift my head and see Lucija looking at LeBeaux. Lu's eyes are open wide, like she's on drugs.

"So, should I finish it? Now?"

LeBeaux grins. "Sure, hun. This one's all yours. I've been training you for this."

In a moment of clarity, I jump at Lucija and pin her on the sofa. A part of me doesn't want to hurt her and be gentle, but the other part wants to grab the knife and stab her heart the way she has stabbed mine. She stares at me, startled.

"What are you going to do? Pull out one of your superhero moves?" That cocky smirk is back on her face. I yank the knife out of her hand. A hint of fear creeps into Lucija's eyes. For a moment I wonder if I'm strong enough to kill her—the one I thought I could rely on, build on. Then I realise what'll hurt her even more.

I spring off the sofa and lunge towards LeBeaux, who has been quietly observing my moves. She seems surprised, like a deer caught in headlights. I suppose she thought I would just kill Lucija and she'd be safe. This is *my* story now. *I* decide what happens next.

I plunge the blade right into LeBeaux's heart without hesitation. She looks at me startled, defenceless. I make it a point to look straight into her eyes the way she has been looking my friends in the eyes before killing them. The knife goes in a lot smoother than I thought it would, piercing her clothes and flesh. Thick blood runs out. I hold the knife firmly and twist a bit. LeBeaux squirms with pain, looking away from me, trying to ignore my stare.

Lucija jumps up and shouts. "No, don't touch her! Get off!" She throws herself at me and starts clawing her nails into my face. I feel the sharp nails hitting my cheeks, and for some reason, it feels more painful than my stomach. We both scream, me in terror, Lucija enraged. I never could have imagined the two of us ending up in this situation. When I see the hate in her eyes, I push my emotions aside again for a moment.

I elbow Lucija in the face so she flops back down on the sofa. I stab LeBeaux again and again and again in the heart until the knife drains the life from her eyes.

I pull out the bloodied knife from her body and immediately point it at Lucija in self-defence. My breathing has become short and shallow. My head is throbbing, following the beat of my heart. I feel empowered now—nobody can stop me. I am getting out of this alive, with Karla by my side.

LeBeaux's body drops like a sad bag of potatoes. Lucija stares at the lifeless body in shock. I know this would be the perfect moment to stab Lucija, but something inside of me stops me from doing so. All those moments we've had together over the past months, they can't all have been fake. There must be good in her somewhere. As I look down at my stomach, which is still bleeding, I decide my best bet is to run away and get help. I'm not dropping the knife this time.

I run towards the staircase as Lucija comes out of her trance and realises I'm gone. As I make it to the top of the staircase, I can hear her yelling like a madman. "Don't you for a second think I'll let you get away! I'll gut you like a pig!"

"Try me!" I run down the staircase and through the hall on the sixth floor. LeBeaux was right, no policemen or guards to be seen anywhere. The building seems empty. Not a soul inside except for Lucija and me. I can tell she isn't far behind me, but I refuse to look back. It'll only slow me down and these stab wounds are slowing me down enough as it is. I'm wondering where to run. Is there a room she doesn't know about? I guess not—I've shown her all the hidden spots as her mentor. Great.

I keep running, down to the fifth floor. She's still right behind me. I feel like she's catching up. The stomach wound is becoming more painful by the second, but I won't give up. No way, not after everything I've been through. Everyone I've lost.

I decide to run to the main entry and keep making my way down the stairs. I'm down to the second floor, but I realise the footsteps above me have stopped. Lucija seems to have taken a different route. I stop for a second and hold on tight to the railing. I notice some dried up blood stains on it. Ingvild. I can't believe I've lost her too. I hope she didn't realise Lucija was behind all of this. It would've hurt her so much. I hope she didn't have to feel too much pain. I feel tears building up, but now is not the time. I'm not out of the doghouse just yet.

I look around me, but no one's to be seen. I hear some muffled voices coming from outside, I wonder if it's the cops ready to burst into the dorms. That is probably wishful thinking though. They haven't exactly been much help to any of us. Perhaps it's the other dorm girls, waiting outside for me. Or the press, they'll probably be here before any police arrive. Shocker.

I notice the sharp pain in my stomach again. I just need to keep moving, so I hold onto the knife and keep running down. I have made it to the first floor. Still no other sounds—or? I hear some murmuring coming from the entry hall. I stop again for a second and catch my breath. I need to save my energy for when Lucija pops up. I know how this goes. I've seen it countless times. This is the moment the deranged serial killer pops out of nowhere and tries to get to the Final Girl. It's too quiet here, so I stay alert, trying to catch some small movement in the shadows around me. I look at the light green doors of the entry hall that cast a diagonal shadow over the eggshell white walls on the left and right, but no-one's there. Not as far as I can tell anyway. I turn my gaze to the left and see the massive paintings looking creepier than ever. It's as if the ghosts behind these paintings have been following us throughout the evening, looking more evil each time I look at them.

I look to my right towards the spiral staircase I just came down from, but nothing is to be seen there either. Maybe there is no jump scare this time around. I could just open these gates behind me and walk out into safety, into another life.

A hand touches my left shoulder. I scream and spin around, holding my knife even more tightly.

"Don't!" Karla screams at me. "Don't hurt me!"

"Karla? What the hell are you doing here? I thought you went outside!"

"I did, but I couldn't lose you again. I went back in the

moment those girls ran out of the halls. I've been looking for you. I don't get what's happening." She takes a step back and scans me. I notice she is analysing my bloodied hand and knife. "Did you? Are you—?"

"No, I'm not the killer! Listen, we have to whisper, please trust me on this one."

She steps closer towards me again. My heart skips a beat, I am so touched she's here. She still makes me feel nervous though, even through all of this mess.

"Okay, alright, then who—?"

"The detective and Lucija. I'll explain later. I killed the detective, but Lucija's still around. She's after me."

"Lu? For real?" She stares at me in disbelief. "But I thought you two were—?"

"I know." A wave of sadness hits me. "I thought so too." She looks down at my stomach. "Oh God, I didn't even notice, I was too caught up in—are you okay? Of course not, stupid question."

"I will be. We just need to get out of here and get help."

"Okay, okay, let's go to the exit. All of the cops left all of a sudden, they were all high fiving each other for some reason."

I roll my eyes. Gullible bunch.

We hear a loud bang coming from the main door.

Karla looks at me, scared. "She's locked it. That must be Lucija, right? How can we get out?"

I try to think. It's becoming harder by the minute. I'm becoming weaker. Somehow my guard is down a bit now that Kara's next to me, but I don't want to be that fool that starts relaxing too much and then gets killed because I'm not paying attention. I toughen up again. "The windows in the yoga room! If we jump out of those, we can make it out to the garden."

Karla nods and we both move towards the yoga room at the end of the first floor. I feel Karla squeezing my hand, and as much as it physically hurts, it feels good to have her by my side again. Her hand feels a lot warmer than mine. My hands are ice cold, even though I feel like the rest of my body is burning up. I need to get help soon; time is running out.

We swing open the room and run straight to the large wooden-panelled windows, running over the yoga mats that are spread out on the floor.

This particular room was always a safe haven for the six of us. We'd come here for after school sports and do pilates or yoga. I love those teachers. They always know how to calm us down when we've had a stressful day at school or when there was some friendship drama going on. They'd dim the lights and light some incense. One of them usually brings her salt lamp for its "healing properties." In a way, I wish they were here now and could help me with some guided breathing exercises. Lord knows I could use them.

A taillight from one of the cars driving by outside hits my eyes. Right, stay focused. Even though the pain in my stomach is only getting worse, I try to open one of the windows, but they're quite big and old.

"Wait, let me," Karla says as she takes over. She forces one of the windows open. It makes a high-pitched noise. I cringe a little. The sound reminds me of chalk being dragged down the blackboard at school.

We hear footsteps down the hallway. We look at each other quickly and signal that it's time to go. Somehow the stakes feel higher right now. I've been taking care of myself so far, but now that Karla is here, I won't lose her. I can't. I try to take a deep breath, but my body is not exactly on board.

"I'll go first so I can catch you. You need to save your strength," Karla whispers. Her empathy touches me in ways I can't even put into words, much needed after Lucija's betrayal.

"Thanks, go, go. She's close!"

Karla jumps out and lands on one of the prickly bushes underneath the window. I can tell she's in a bit of pain but shrugs it off immediately. I look out of the window. It's dark outside, just some old streetlights at the road behind the garden that add a warm sepia-coloured glow to the surrounding trees. Weeping willows. Of course.

"Liv, come on, jump!" she shouts a little too loudly. I hear the footsteps down the hallway, Lucija's getting closer. I try to pull myself up, but it hurts a lot. I don't know if I've got it in me. She can tell I'm struggling. I don't want her to see how much pain I'm in.

"You've got this, Livvy. I'm not leaving without you again!" Her eyes show me how determined she is to make it out of here with me. I pull it together and lift myself up to the windowpane. Karla is waiting for me just beneath. Good thing we're on the first floor and not on the seventh anymore. The moment I want to jump down, I see a dark figure standing next to Karla behind one of the bushes. An unsettling feeling kicks in. "Karla! Watch out!"

"What's wrong?" Karla manically looks around her but can't see her. Lucija jumps right on top of her. I hold my breath and nervously clench my fists.

Karla screams and lifts her head, giving Lucija a hard, effective head bump. Karla pushes Lucija off her and stands up as Lucija falls on the lawn. A soft landing—this won't slow her down enough. Karla quickly looks up at me for reassurance. The faintest smile. At this moment I can tell she also doesn't want to show me she's in pain. But I know her, and she knows me.

"Run, Karla, run! I'm right behind you!"

Lucija seems a bit dizzy but does manage to get up. She runs after Karla without even looking up at me. I look behind me into the yoga room and continue hearing footsteps. Who else is out there?

When I look back, I can see Karla and Lucija are running from the garden towards the main door.

I tighten my stomach muscles and jump out of the window, still holding onto the knife. As I land, one of the branches pierces my stomach right where I've been stabbed, and I feel like I am about to pass out. As I lay here, I smell the thin droplets of dew on the lawn. The juxtaposition with the smell of fresh blood hits like a brick. Like, a really large brick. An ugly one.

I am feeling nauseous, but I know Karla is in danger. A part of me wants to just lay here until—at some point in the distant future—the cops show up, but I can't let Karla down. She didn't ask for any of this. I amp myself up as I stand up—the wobbliest of stances—and I start running, or walk-running to be more honest, after Karla and Lucija.

"Hey Lu!" I yell at her. Lucija's posture seems startled. She stops her chase in the middle of the garden and looks back at me.

"What?" she replies, the darkest of grins.

I can see Karla sprinting away without looking back, getting out of sight. I hope she makes it. I was hoping she would stay, but I get it, this is between Lucija and me. I exhale and feel a sense of relief for Karla. I immediately tense up again as I look Lucija in the eyes. *This is it.*

"You forgot something."

She seems a bit curious and starts walking towards me. My

heartbeat speeds up. Something about this walk is completely different to what I've seen over the last months. It's almost as if something demonic has taken over. This primaeval, gangly walk. Her arms and legs seem longer and thinner than before. I know it's my own warped vision of her, but she almost doesn't look human.

"What is it? Do you want a more fleshed out motive?" She smiles diabolically as she continues walking towards me.

"No. It's not that." I try to keep it together. *Now is not the time to show her you're scared. Stay calm. Stay composed. Don't show her you're scared.*

We are standing right in front of each other. It's just her and me in the middle of the dark garden, metres away from the entrance of Europea Halls. There is a slight drizzle, and the garden looks a bit misty. It sort of feels like we're in the middle of a damp, Gothic swamp.

"Then what is it? Some Act Three shit you haven't bored me with yet?"

"No, it's simple." Lucija looks confused, or it could be irritation as well. I know she doesn't like it when I know more than her. She's always been a bit arrogant, now that I think about it.

I grab the knife from behind my back and jump towards her. "Your knife. What's a killer without a knife?" But I stumble and lose my balance as my body gives in. Lucija grabs the knife from me as I am trying to find my balance and stabs my right leg. It all goes so fast. I try to look for something else to hurt her with, but these tiny bushes and dried out flowers—thank you January—are not exactly lethal weapons. She hasn't stabbed me too deeply. My awkward balancing act made it hard for her to aim properly. This isn't how I planned it, but I'm still here.

I straighten my back, even though it hurts like hell, and show Lucija how confident I supposedly am. She is holding the knife and standing right in front of me. A small gust of cold wind caresses my cheeks. It makes me feel stronger.

It feels like we are in some sort of Western duel. Only in Westerns both characters have a weapon. I need to figure something else out. Lucija starts smiling again.

"What is it, Liv? This scenario wasn't in your playbook?"

"No, it's not that. It's just that—"

"What?" she shouts back at me.

"I thought I had killed LeBeaux." I look behind Lucija and pretend to see the detective. Lucija instinctively looks behind her. I can't believe that actually worked. I jump forward with all my might and steal the knife from her. Lucija looks back at me, still fully confused, as I plummet the blade into the right side of her throat, just underneath her right ear. The blood chaotically spews out at me. She still looks puzzled and tries to reach for the knife but falls to her knees.

"Aim for the head, remember?" I step a bit closer to her and tower over her menacingly. This time, I'm the one with the long arms and legs. This time, I'm the diabolical humanoid. I look down at her as she looks up. I'm not sure what she's thinking or what she's feeling. Remorse? I don't think she's able to feel those kinds of feelings. She's probably just scared of dying. Just like all of us. Just like LeBeaux before I stabbed her.

"You want your knife, Lu?"

She nods, almost like a desperate toddler. I swing the knife and stab her in the throat again, this time in the left side of her neck. The blood flows down onto the grass, diluted by the raindrops which are becoming thicker by the minute.

"Here it is."

I slowly slice her throat from left to right until she drops onto the lawn into a pool of rain and blood.

Lucija's head tilts back in an unnatural way, showing the huge gash caused by the knife. By me, I should say. Her lower body is still convulsing a bit, but her almost-severed head isn't.

I can see Lucija exhaling her final breath. I lift up her left arm and check her pulse, just to be sure. No more rookie mistakes. She's gone. I want to sit down next to her and hold her hand, but all I feel right now is pity and hate towards her. Because of her, all my best friends are dead. Gone. And for what? What crime did we ever commit?

I wonder where Karla is. I decide to walk towards the main door of the halls. Every single step hurts more than the previous. It's as if I had forgotten about the pain for a second, but it's hitting me twice as hard now. I'm almost at the end of the garden now; the main gates are just a couple of steps away. I hear voices and sirens in the distance. The cops are here. Finally. Safety.

I look back to make sure Lucija's dead. She's dead alright. The moment I look in front of me again, I'm being pushed down to the ground.

LeBeaux is standing in front of me. She kicks me in the stomach and ribs. I let out an intense scream. The moment I fall down, she takes my knife. I can tell she's as badly hurt as I am.

I should've checked her pulse too. Guess I'm not the connoisseur I thought I was.

She looks absolutely terrifying. Blood all over her, even in her blonde hair, streaks of murky dark maroon. Her face covered in it.

"Did you think you'd get rid of me that easily?" She kicks me again. I try to stand up, but she instantly puts her right foot on my shoulder and pushes me down onto the grass.

"To be fair, you did make it pretty far. I didn't think you'd have it in you. Maybe you should've joined my team instead of Lucija."

She looks at Lucija's body. I expect some kind of emotion, but it doesn't seem to hurt or faze her. I look around for any kind of weapon but find nothing. It doesn't seem like LeBeaux has any extra weapons on her either as I scan her pockets. This feels hopeless. I don't want to cry, but the tears start rolling down my cold cheeks. I thought I had made it.

"Now don't get all melodramatic please—I've dealt with that at the station for years. You're not that special." She looks back at Lucija and grins.

"What?" I ask her.

"Guess I'm the Final Girl after all. The detective, sole sur-vivor." LeBeaux stares at the knife and redirects her gaze at me.

"And to think you almost made it. So close. And Miss Motive? Don't believe for a *second* things are as straightforward as they seem. Guess you'll never find out the real reason behind all of this. Any last words, Miss Poland?"

I close my eyes, because I don't want to see what's about to happen, but when I hear rustling sounds coming from the bushes, I open them up again. LeBeaux is lunging the knife towards my head, but at that exact time an axe slices right through LeBeaux's neck. Her blood splatters all over my face and neck. I didn't think I still had any vocal chords left, but another scream comes out of me, rolling out from deep within me. Her head rolls down the lawn and keeps tumbling forward like a deformed bowling ball. The rest of her body falls down a mere second later.

Karla appears behind LeBeaux. "You always have to aim for the head in slashers." Karla says, smiling.

I don't know how to react.

"You didn't think I'd just leave you behind again, right? But I needed a weapon. So, I smashed the glass of the safety box at the entry hall to get the axe and came right back for you. Seems like a lot can happen in a minute."

It sure felt like more than a minute, but I guess you lose track of time or reality in situations like these.

Karla's never this chirpy, but then again, I guess the circumstances aren't exactly normal. She pulls me up and puts her right arm around my shoulders. I try to bite back the pain, but tears continue rolling down my bloodied cheeks.

"Are you okay, Livvy?" I can tell she instantly regrets asking me that question again.

I look at the bodies of LeBeaux and Lucija. "No, I'm not. But I will be."

We both start walking, or wobbling rather in my case, towards the entry hall. To my surprise, I see three police cars on standby. The cops run towards me and help out Karla. "We've got you, miss, you're okay now!"

"Thanks, you were such a big help tonight," I say sarcastically. I can't help myself.

Karla snickers. "By the way, Livvy, lovely dress. Only you can look elegant through all of this." We squeeze each other's hand and smile at each other. I can finally exhale.

Karla and I are being directed towards one of the police cars. I notice an ambulance at the back of the parking lot.

I point towards it. "Excuse me, why is there an ambulance?"

The policeman who is carrying me answers. "There was another survivor. She's in very bad shape, but she might make it. Why don't you take a seat, miss, so we can -"

I push the cop to the side and start limping towards the ambulance. The back door is still half open.

"Excuse me, can I—Who is in there?"

The medic looks at me and points towards my stomach.

"Are you alright, miss? We should get that checked immediately. Didn't the police tell you to come here?"

I sigh. "No, they sure didn't."

He opens the door to the back of the van. I see her. It's Ingvild. She is lying on a stretcher. Her face is covered with one of those oxygen mask thingies.

"Ing, you've made it!" My cheeks hurt as I pull out the biggest smile. I jump towards her and lean in for a hug.

The medic pulls me back. "Easy there, your friend is still very weak. She's been stabbed multiple times and thrown down the stairs." Ingvild looks at me and weakly lifts her hand for a small wave.

"Ing! Are you okay?" More tears roll down my cheeks.

She makes an "okay" sign with her thumb and index finger.

Chapter 27

EPILOGUE

OLIWIA

I can't believe it's been a year. I also can't believe we all decided to stay at Europea Halls. My initial instinct was to run far away and never come back. But something about facing your demons and all that encouraged me to stay. All of us wanted to—Ingvild, Karla, and me. After the initial shock of it all, a lot more details about Lucija came to light. Karel told us that it turned out Matej had been chatting with an old school friend of Lucija's who was warning him about her aggressive behaviour back in Croatia. Matej told Karel that he wanted to come warn me, but as I was always around Lucija, he needed to go talk to one of the girls from the group who was alone. When he saw Alzbeta's story on Instagram, he noticed she was in her mansion on her own, so he thought it would be best to talk to Alzy first. He had been trying to warn us all, but Lucija had fooled us. All of us. And LeBeaux, well, that thing she told me at the end? I still don't get it. What other motive was there?

The months after the incident, my mom pushed me into therapy and I have to say, in retrospect, I'm glad she did. I noticed I had been putting up my walls and didn't trust anyone around me anymore. Even Karla at first. We have had a bit of a bumpy ride, but we're still here.

"In deep thought, are we?" Karel smiles at me.

"Sorry, I was just—reflecting, I guess."

"About Lucija?" he asks, empathically.

"Yes, about all of it. I'm sorry, we've rehashed this so many times. It's just—it's been a year today. And the four of us being together here, in my dorm room, feels quite symbolic, you know?"

Ingvild looks at me with sad eyes and grabs one of my hands. "We know. We're still here though. We've made it out alive. It sure took a lot of hospital visits and physiotherapy, but hey, nobody messes with us."

Karla takes my other hand. "Exactly, maybe we should do some sort of ritual to commemorate Alzy, Marieke, Ayat, Matej, and all the other people who died last year."

I like that idea.

"We can make it an annual thing," she continues. "But a positive ritual, something uplifting."

Karel smiles at Ingvild and strokes her back. Now *that* one I definitely didn't see coming.

"So, when exactly did you two get together?" I ask both of them. Ingvild looks a bit shy but decides to explain before Karel gets a chance to. "It has been going on for some months, but we didn't know how you'd react. I guess we found comfort in each other. He drove me to physio almost every Monday and helped me with the entire revalidation process."

Karel smiles. He looks genuinely happy. "I basically taught her how to walk again."

Ing scoffs. "As if, get over yourself!" They wink at each other.

"She's been my rock through all of this. Losing Matej has been rough on me. It's been rough on all of us of course, but I mean, he was my buddy. Not many people can actually understand what it's like, losing someone that way." His voice breaks.

Karla replies: "The bromance was real with you two, wasn't it?"

Karel laughs loudly. Ingvild hushes him. "Quiet! You're not even supposed to be in the halls! Do you want us all to get expelled or something?"

"We've gone through worse," I say to all of them and smile. There's still a sense of sadness in the room, but I feel some sort of hope too. Maybe we can move forward together, the four of us. We've already made plans to go to Budapest together in two weeks.

I get a text message. I quickly grab my phone out of my jeans pocket and look at the screen.

Unknown number: *Didn't you listen to the detective? You should've joined the team. There are more of us. We've been training for this. Happy anniversary. We'll see you all very soon.*

About the Author

As someone who grew up in the 90s, Alan Shivers fell in love with the campy, MTV-era type of slashers. He mixes these 90s elements with modern European city vibes in his trilogy Europea Halls. Based in Brussels, Belgium.

Subscribe to my newsletter:

✉ https://mailchi.mp/b57ece14816e/europea-halls-trilogy

Also by Alan Shivers

Europea Halls 2: A Summer in Budapest
When the survivors of Europea Halls' massacre go on a summer trip to Budapest, they are in dire need of a good time.

However, when one of their new friends gets brutally killed, it seems like the past is still hunting them.

OUT ON January 20, 2024.

Europea Halls 3
When the survivors of the summer massacre in Budapest are forced to go to Brussels, they will learn the hard way that the final chapter of a Slasher Trilogy always goes back to the beginning.

OUT 2024.

Printed in Great Britain
by Amazon

37046839R00101